Gavin Stoddart was born in Leeds but has lived in Nigeria, Sierra Leone, Pakistan, India, Brazil and Russia. He now calls London home.

Gavin started his writing career at *Where & When,* an arts and entertainment magazine for Yorkshire. Since then, he has been published in titles ranging from the *FT* and *Global Tax Weekly* to the *South London Press.*

Seasons in the City is his first venture into fiction.

Gavin lists his hobbies as scuba diving, photography, playing tennis (badly) and travelling to the coldest places he can find.

To E, without whom this book would not exist.

Gavin Stoddart

SEASONS IN THE CITY

Austin Macauley Publishers

LONDON · CAMBRIDGE · NEW YORK · SHARJAH

Copyright © Gavin Stoddart 2025

The right of Gavin Stoddart to be identified as author of this work has been asserted by the author in accordance with sections 77 and 78 of the Copyright, Designs and Patents Act 1988.

All rights reserved. No part of this publication may be reproduced, stored in a retrieval system, or transmitted in any form or by any means, electronic, mechanical, photocopying, recording, or otherwise, without the prior permission of the publishers.

Any person who commits any unauthorised act in relation to this publication may be liable to criminal prosecution and civil claims for damages.

This is a work of fiction. Names, characters, businesses, places, events, locales, and incidents are either the products of the author's imagination or used in a fictitious manner. Any resemblance to actual persons, living or dead, or actual events is purely coincidental.

A CIP catalogue record for this title is available from the British Library.

ISBN 9781035898800 (Paperback)
ISBN 9781035898817 (ePub e-book)

www.austinmacauley.com

First Published 2025
Austin Macauley Publishers Ltd®
1 Canada Square
Canary Wharf
London
E14 5AA

Table of Contents

Summer   **9**
    The Fox   *11*
    UFO   *20*
    Anna's Hummingbird   *28*

Autumn   **39**
    They Are Down There   *41*
    Judgement Day   *65*
    Moving On   *74*

Winter   **83**
    A Miscalculation   *85*
    Chloe   *91*
    Border Dispute   *96*

Spring   **103**
    One Day in the Life of Maria Popescu   *105*
    Superstar   *113*
    The Sommelier's Second Epiphany   *123*

Summer

The Fox

It started one July morning when Andy came into the kitchen to make breakfast. Looking through the window, he thought he could see something. Was there an animal under the cherry tree at the end of the garden? It only took him a few seconds to be sure. There was. No doubt about it. A creature of some sort was lying there amongst the hellebores. But what was it? From where he was standing, Andy couldn't make it out.

Andy decided to take a closer look. He opened the back door, walked a few steps across the patio, and stopped to observe the semi-hidden animal. Now it was clear. The crouched shape lying flat against the ground, its head resting on its paws, and its tail sticking out behind it, was a fox.

No surprise seeing a fox in the garden. It was not as if there was any shortage of them in London. Andy and Ella regularly saw them on the local streets and in the garden. Usually, the encounters at home took place in the evenings after it started to get dark, occasionally in the mornings before it was completely light. If Andy and Ella remained undetected, the fox would do its thing for a while and then casually wander off. If the fox spotted them, it would scamper away, jumping onto the low wall that separated their home from Number 86 or disappearing through a hole in the fence to the garden on the other side.

Even if they had never seen one, Ella and Andy would have known foxes were regular visitors to the garden from the evidence left behind. With depressing frequency, they would find a discarded trophy from a rubbish bin robbery or the remains of a dismembered victim. The abandoned meals, especially the unwanted parts of dead birds and rats were sometimes a little gruesome. They were always revolting to clear up. But, for sheer annoyance, the earthworks were worse.

Although it was perfectly possible for the foxes to jump onto and over the wall at the bottom of the garden, for some reason, they had decided they wanted to dig a tunnel under it. As a result, there was an ongoing battle between the homeowners and the invaders. Two or three times a month, the foxes would decide that the best use of their night was to get on with their guerilla excavations. The next day Andy would carefully undo their hard work and return the flowerbed to its original state. The war had been going on for years. There was no sign of a truce in the making.

Today's encounter was unlike any previous encounter. It wasn't just the time of day (sunlight was already flooding into the garden) the other, more worrying difference, was that the fox refused to retreat. Even as Andy took another couple of steps towards the back of the garden, the enemy held its position. By the time Andy got to the bridge over the pond, he hadn't seen a single twitch from the form lurking amongst the plants. Although the fox was still a good three meters away, Andy had never been so close to one before. What should he do next?

One part of Andy told him he should chase the fox away. If he didn't, it would only get bolder. He had to show the invader that the garden was his territory. On the other hand, weren't foxes dangerous? Didn't they attack humans when cornered? Hadn't Andy read something about one killing a baby in Bromley?

Andy decided that discretion was the better part of valour. He retreated to the safety of the house.

After a council of war with Ella, Andy returned to the garden, hoping the fox had already left, but carrying a golf umbrella all the same. No luck. The fox was still occupying the territory it had claimed. Andy moved slowly towards it. He crossed the bridge and took a couple more steps before stopping. Now he was a mere metre away from the enemy. Andy sensed something was wrong. The fox should have run by now. Perhaps it was ill. Andy reached out with the umbrella and gently prodded it. No reaction. Then the realisation came. The fox was dead.

Relieved, Andy retreated once again.

This time, the subject of conversation with Ella was the dead body. What should they do with it? In this heat, it would soon start decomposing. Ella suggested burying it, but Andy didn't want a large dead fox under the flowerbeds or lawn. Wouldn't it smell? And, what if the other foxes dug it up? Ella and Andy discussed their options. After a couple of minutes, Ella suggested speaking to someone from the council. Andy liked that idea. He said he would call them as soon as he got to work.

After half an hour pressing keys on his phone and listening to recorded messages, Andy got through to Southwark Pest Control. The conversation started well. Andy explained that he had a fox in the garden and that he would like it removed. The person on the other end of the line was sympathetic and agreed that foxes were a problem across the borough. Andy and the pest control person then agreed on a time for one of the team to come round. "Of course," the voice at the other end of the phone added, "with a fox you need to know we can't guarantee we will be able to catch it."

"I don't think that will be a problem," responded Andy, "it's dead."

There was a long silence. Then the voice spoke again, "I am afraid that changes things." Over the next few minutes, Andy learned that although Pest Control spent most of their time killing unwanted creatures, they were not able to deal with anything that was dead before they arrived. "You need Refuse Disposal and Recycling for that. I would transfer you, but it will probably be quicker if you just call again." The conversation ended.

After another half hour of recorded messages, Andy was through to Refuse Disposal and Recycling. He wasn't going to make the same mistake again and so, from the beginning, he made it very clear that the fox he was discussing was dead. Not that it mattered. Because, as it turned out, Andy wasn't ready for the critical question when it came, "Where did you say the body is?"

"In our garden," he innocently replied.

"Ohh! That's a problem," he was told. "We can't remove a dead body from private property. If it was in the street, that would be a different matter." In a final attempt to help, the voice asked, "You're not council tenants by any chance, are you? If you are, then the garden is council property and we can send someone." Andy admitted he wasn't a council tenant. Then, unfortunately, the fox was not the council's responsibility. Andy and Ella would have to deal with it themselves.

Looking for some guidance, Andy asked, "If you can't move it, who can?"

"A private company might do it," he was told. "I can give you the number of the Braintree Biohazard Removal Company. We sometimes use them." Andy wrote the number down. Then the speaker added, "Or if you want, you can take it to the recycling centre on the Old Kent Road yourself."

Andy didn't fancy traipsing around South London with a fox that had died of unknown causes in the back of his car. He decided to call the number he had been given. It didn't take long to confirm that the Braintree Biohazard Removal Company could indeed remove not only a dead fox but almost any kind of dead animal. After answering various questions about the body and its location, Andy asked about costs. The response he received convinced Andy that the Braintree Biohazard Company must be planning a very elaborate funeral for the deceased. He almost asked them what they were going to use for the casket. Teak perhaps? But he resisted the temptation. Instead, he simply said he would call back after discussing things with his wife. He knew he was lying. Ella would never agree to spend that much money if the alternative was a short drive down the Old Kent Road.

When Andy spoke to Ella, the conversation went as he expected. Ella had no intention of shelling out money when they could sort the problem out for free. They planned the removal operation for the next day. The recycling centre opened at eight. If Andy and Ella got up an hour earlier than usual, it would be tight, but they could still get to work on time.

The next morning, after checking that the body had not miraculously disappeared overnight, Andy and Ella ate breakfast and got ready for their first venture into animal undertaking. They would have looked the part in their sombre office suits if it wasn't for the bright yellow washing-up gloves they had also donned. They ventured into the garden and over the bridge carrying a large black bin bag. As they approached the fox, they both noticed a few patches of what looked like mange along its back. Andy was pleased they had the gloves.

Feeling squeamish but putting on his most courageous face, Andy got to work. He tried hard not to think about fleas or the diseases that might be lurking in the fox's body. First, he rolled the black bag back on itself. Then he slid the vixen's nose into the end of the bag. As he unrolled and lifted, the body started to slide into the bag. Ella and Andy had both assumed that there would be plenty of room for one dead fox in a large bin bag. They were wrong. Rigour mortis had set in. Instead of curling into a ball as it slid into the bag, the fox remained rigidly stiff. When Andy finished, the fox's face and front paws were hidden from sight inside the bag, but its tail and back end poked out of the bag, pointing skywards. Ella got another bag. That and some carefully applied Sellotape were enough to turn the fox into a neatly wrapped parcel.

Andy gingerly carried the package through the house and out into the street in front. There, he placed it in the boot of the car after first checking the plastic sheet he had laid there was still in place.

When they arrived at the recycling centre, the conversation didn't go as Andy and Ella had expected. Andy stopped by the ramp and wound down the window to speak to the man standing there. "What have you got?" Andy replied honestly. The look that came over the man's face told Andy the conversation was going to take a turn he wouldn't like, "A what?" asked the council worker incredulously.

"A dead fox," repeated Andy.

The man's expression stayed the same. After a long silence, he replied, "Well, you can't bring that in here."

Andy asked why and then explained what he had been told on the phone. Ella pleaded and then asked what they were to do with the body if they couldn't leave it at the recycling centre. Andy repeated what he had been told. Ella tried pleading again. Nothing they said changed anything. The recycling centre didn't accept dead bodies. That was it. The fox was going to be keeping Andy and Ella company for a while longer.

Andy started to panic. What were they going to do? Take the body to work? Drop it off at home? But, then what? As they drove, Ella and Andy discussed options. The back garden burial was on the agenda once again. Ella thought they should give it a go. Andy was still sceptical. Before they had come to an agreement, Ella spotted a dustbin wagon making its rounds. "Stop," she shouted at Andy, "Maybe they'll take it." Ella and Andy, both knew it was a long shot, but they were desperate. Andy explained the situation to the driver and asked if they could put the neatly wrapped fox in with the rest of the bags. The answer was a firm, "No". Health and safety didn't allow refuse collectors to collect dead pets. Ready to try anything, Ella quibbled that the fox wasn't a pet. No luck.

The same rule applied to any dead animal a household might have to dispose of. Ella wondered if it might help if she pointed out that half the leftover food that into bins was bits of dead animals. She thought better of it. Ella and Andy got back in the car with the fox.

The interrupted conversation continued. Andy was trying to convince Ella that the only thing they could do was to pay the ridiculous charge the Braintree Biohazard Removal Company was asking for. Ella was not ready to give up so easily. Something in the conversation with the driver of the dustbin wagon had got her thinking. "Tell me again what the people in the Recycling and Waste Department said to you. The bit about not collecting dead animals from private property." Andy explained once again that the council would only deal with dead animals found on public land, anything on private land was the owner's responsibility. "So, they are set up to deal with dead bodies, they just choose not to deal with ones on private land," Ella commented. Andy nodded. Ella continued, "So if we accidentally left the boot of the car open and the fox fell out onto the road, the council would collect it?" Andy had to admit that seemed to be the case. But wasn't it a bit anti-social to leave a dead fox in the middle of the road? "Perhaps we could accidentally drop it near a rubbish bin," Ella suggested as a compromise.

It took them five minutes to find somewhere suitably out of sight of CCTV cameras. Andy parked and got the package out of the boot. Should he unwrap it? That way the refuse collectors could see what they were dealing with. But Andy didn't really fancy doing that job without gloves. Besides, a dead fox on the street could frighten a passing child. No, best to leave the fox in its black plastic winding sheets. Andy went over to the bin. The body was still as stiff as when he had wrapped it. If he lay it flat on the ground, it would stick out too far. Better prop it up against the side of the bin.

Andy walked back to the car and got in. Somehow it seemed a little disrespectful to leave the fox, who by now felt almost like a part of the family, balancing on her nose beside a council rubbish bin. But they had to get to work. Andy drove off with just one backward glance.

UFO

It was part of Lucy's daily routine to spend half an hour with a good book and a well-diluted G&T before she started to cook her evening meal. Although she normally had just one G&T, that Tuesday, Lucy was on her second. A strong second. It had been one of those days. After what she had been through, she felt she deserved something to reduce the stress.

Her morning had started with an unexpected phone call. Unexpected phone calls these days were invariably bad news. It might be an ill neighbour asking Lucy to do their shopping for them, a friend who had been taken into hospital, or, worst of all, an invitation to another funeral. This time it had been the news that her cousin Paul had died the night before. It wasn't really a surprise – older than her, he was in his early nineties and had been ill for a while. None of that stopped the news from being a shock.

Over the last sixty years, Lucy had only seen Paul occasionally. But as children and young adults, they had been close. At one point, she even thought he was going to ask her to marry him. That never happened, and they had drifted apart. As it turned out, Lucy never married. She sometimes wondered what life would have been like with a husband, but somehow, never with any real regret.

Did thinking about Paul distract her? Perhaps. Whatever the reason, just before lunch, Lucy caught her foot on a turned-up carpet corner, tripped, and fell. After a quick assessment of the damage, she decided she had been lucky. Nothing was broken. She had a graze on her knee and might end up with a black eye from the bump on her forehead. Other than that, in her opinion, and she was a trained nurse, there was nothing wrong with her. No need to pull the emergency cord. No need to trouble the warden. She could perfectly well deal with the situation herself.

Never marrying and forty years working in the NHS teaches you resilience. Ever since she started to train as a nurse, she had lived alone. First in a room in the hospital then in a small flat of her own. It hadn't taken her long to appreciate the positive side of having her own space to return to at the end of a hard day. Eventually, she couldn't imagine it any other way. After she retired, she continued to live on her own for another twenty years. Only when she sensed her physical and mental abilities were starting to decline, did she sell up and move into sheltered housing. It suited her well. She had her own ground-floor flat and could arrange her life as she liked. At the same time, she knew, if it was ever needed, help was just one pull of a cord away.

The third piece of misfortune that Tuesday (it did seem, she thought, bad luck always came in threes), might seem trivial to you, but to Lucy, it was almost worse than the tumble she had taken – it started to rain. Not just rain, a real storm with thunder and lightning. None of that upset Lucy. Almost the opposite. The energy of a strong storm somehow invigorated her. Even during a normal downpour, Lucy enjoyed sitting warm and cosy in her living room listening to the patter of rain against the windows and watching the droplets run down the glass. It was the timing that upset her. A midday storm meant no walk after lunch.

If Lucy's post-lunch walk was the second mainstay of her daily routine, the third was her regular mealtimes. As a former nurse, Lucy liked routine not only in the way she ordered her days but also in the way, she structured her week. When she was working, it had helped her keep the ward functioning properly. In retirement, it kept her sane. shopping on Monday and Friday, Yoga on Tuesday and Thursday, cleaning on Wednesday, friends over on Saturday and Sunday to rest – every activity assigned its proper time.

That Tuesday, the normal routine had been completely disrupted. After receiving the bad news, she hadn't felt up to her yoga class and had skipped it. Then she missed her walk. By the time she finished her third gin and tonic (it seemed appropriate to have a third, if bad things came in threes why shouldn't good things also?) she was a little disorientated. She looked at her watch. It was already quarter to seven, a full half-hour after she normally started to cook. There was no way dinner was going to be on the table by seven. That couldn't be helped. But she should start cooking now.

As she went to make dinner, Lucy wasn't expecting another surprise. But as she walked through the kitchen door, she saw it, there just outside the back door. At first, Lucy thought it was a reflection or some other trick of the lights. But no, through the glass panels, she could see it quite clearly, hanging in the air. Later, when she thought about it, Lucy told herself the best way to describe the object would be to say it was a sphere the colour of a gas flame. At the time, she was too startled to think anything clearly. She froze, her hand resting on the light switch which, in her surprise, she had forgotten to turn on.

Lucy stared at the object. The object stayed perfectly still. Even so, she found it hard, in the dark, to judge its size or how far away it was. Lucy decided to investigate. She flicked the light on and started to move towards the outside door. It was a surprise for her to see the object mirror her movement. Perhaps it was responding to the light. Perhaps it wanted to get a better look at her. A couple of hesitant steps later, Lucy stopped. She half expected the object to do the same. But, no, it continued to move slowly forwards.

Soon the shining sphere was only a few centimetres from the metal frame of the door. Lucy could see it with absolute clarity. It was smaller than a tennis ball, probably just a little larger than an egg. It seemed to shimmer and at the same time had a pale translucent quality. Lucy couldn't help thinking that, if she tried hard enough, she might be able to see through it. Any fear she had been feeling was gone. The blue glow was somehow very calming. *Like a nightlight*, she thought. Now she was curious. What would the object do when it reached the door? Would it turn and continue its journey along the wall? Would it stop? Would it bump into the glass? If it did, would it damage the glass? Would it damage itself?

Lucy didn't have to wait long to find out. The object reached the door. What happened next was completely unexpected. The object didn't stick to any of the scenarios Lucy had run through her mind. Instead, it just carried straight on travelling through one of the panes of glass without any apparent damage to the door or itself.

Lucy now wondered if she was imagining things. Perhaps she shouldn't have had that third G&T. Perhaps it was the bump on the head. Was she concussed? She didn't know what she thought. The object seemed real enough. But was it? All the while she kept on watching. The object was now inside the house rather than safely outside, she was feeling nervous again. What would it do next? Would it come after her?

Lucy needn't have worried. The object continued slowly in a straight line until it reached the stove. Over the hob, it slowed and almost stopped. Then it changed direction. Speeding up again, it moved in a spiralling downward circle around and into the centre of the hob. The object reached the surface and continued its descent, disappearing into the body of the stove. A second later, Lucy heard a muffled sound like a small explosion. Then silence.

Lucy found herself blinking and shaking her head. Had she really just seen what she had just seen? Without the object there in front of her, she was less and less certain that the object was real. She remembered that time in A&E when the ambulance crew brought in a man convinced, he had seen Martians in his house. It was only after he had gone to his neighbours for help, and they had called the police that anybody discovered he had fallen off a ladder earlier that day and had been drinking medicinal whiskeys ever since. Perhaps she was in a similar state.

Or perhaps not. Maybe she wasn't imagining things. Perhaps it really was what it looked like, a UFO. If so, was it still there in the oven? She hadn't noticed it come out. So, it should still be there. What to do next? Should she call the police? Or would the fire brigade be better? She imagined how the conversation might go:

"I would like to report a UFO."
"And where is this UFO?"
"In my oven, can you send somebody to investigate?"
"Madam, have you been drinking?"
"Well..."

No, she wasn't going to risk being taken to the nearest mental health facility. She would have a look in the oven herself first. If the UFO was still there, she would call the police. If not, that was the end of the matter.

Plucking up her courage, Lucy went over to the oven. Standing carefully to one side in case the UFO suddenly flew out, Lucy gingerly opened the oven door. Nothing happened. She looked inside. There was nothing there. That settled it, she wasn't calling anybody. The incident was over.

But it wasn't. The mystery was still unsolved, and Lucy couldn't get it out of her mind. What had just happened? Lucy could think of nothing else for the rest of the evening. She tried to distract herself by making dinner. But she couldn't get the stove to work. She had to settle for crackers and cheese. All the time she kept on thinking.

She tried to be logical. There were two possibilities. Either a UFO had just flown through her kitchen door, descended into her oven and disappeared into thin air or her brain wasn't functioning properly. What was more likely? The UFO had seemed real enough but, isn't that the way with hallucinations? She had suffered an emotional shock and a blow to the head earlier that day, not to mention consuming half her normal weekly ration of alcohol in the hour immediately before the incident. Any one of those factors could trigger an episode. With all three in play, especially at her age, she had to admit that the medical explanation seemed more probable than the extra-terrestrial one. What were the implications? If she was losing her grasp on reality, would she be allowed to continue to live on her own? Would they insist on her moving into a home? Her freedom was important to Lucy. Given the facts, she didn't assess her chances as good if she told anybody. She wasn't going to risk it. She would keep quiet and see how things went.

Apart from the oven, which continued to refuse to work, everything was outwardly normal over the next couple of days. Lucy didn't see any UFOs, Martians, or pixies. She told herself this should be reassuring. Somehow it wasn't. Variations of the same thoughts she had that Tuesday evening kept coming to her. What was the truth? Had she seen a UFO? Had it perhaps been Paul's spirit paying her a final visit? Was she going out of her mind? Having ruled out the possibility of telling anybody about the incident, the only person listening to Lucy's questions was Lucy herself. And she didn't have the answers. The task was impossible. How could she take an independent view of her own state of mental health?

"Forget it," she told herself. "Stick to your normal routine and don't think about it." Lucy stuck to her normal routine as best possible. She ate her meals on time, did her cleaning, and went to Yoga. But it was a losing battle. She was distracted during the lessons and couldn't concentrate on her book when she got home. She couldn't help thinking and the more she thought, the more she worried.

Things changed on Friday.

Lucy, determined to follow her normal routine, went shopping straight after breakfast exactly as normal. But inside her head, things were still not normal. Between looking out for the cheapest deals and best cuts of meat, Lucy could think of nothing except the UFO and the events of that Tuesday evening. On her way home, she picked up a copy of the South London Press at her local newsagent as she always did. Back home, with her mid-morning coffee by her side, she sat down to read the newspaper.

A headline on the third page caught Lucy's attention: *'Freak Weather Brings Ball Lightning to Bromley'*. Under it, there was a blurred black-and-white picture of something that looked very much like her UFO. She quickly skimmed through the article. The picture had been taken by a reader on Tuesday. Unsure what he had seen, he had sent it to the paper. The consensus, supported by some comments from a meteorologist was that it must have been ball lightning. After a few lines about the phenomenon and previous sightings in London, the article asked anybody who had seen something similar to call the author of the article, Mark Jones.

Smiling for the first time in three days, Lucy picked up the phone. She had somebody to talk to. She was going to tell Mr Jones everything she had seen.

Anna's Hummingbird

For almost as long as he could remember, Bill had been the assumed reinsurance clerk for a large insurance company. His routine never changed. He arrived promptly at nine and started to work through his tasks for the day. From twelve thirty to one thirty, he took precisely one hour for lunch when he ate a sandwich at his desk and did the Crusader Crossword in the Express. To avoid stress, he kept interaction with his colleagues to a minimum and dealt with each item on his to-do list carefully and methodically. Somebody else might have finished the work in half the time but his slow pace meant he always had things to do until five when he left as promptly as he arrived.

No one complained about his work. Far from it – he never made mistakes. At the same time, they never offered him the Deputy Chief Accountant position. That didn't bother Bill too much. He liked things the way they were. It was comforting facing the same issues and coming up with the same solutions week after week. Even if the money was better, a promotion would also have meant more stress.

Bill lived far enough from the centre of town for it to cost him a fortune to get to work but not far enough to escape the sprawl of suburbia. At home, things were no more exciting than at work. Watching Palace at the weekend was an exception. That and going down to the Victory any night he could get away from his wife, Anna. He didn't complain. Actually, all in all, when he bothered to think about it, he was pretty content with life. It was just that sometimes, somewhere at the back of his mind, he was aware of a half-suppressed feeling that there ought to be more.

Bill's favourite time of day, apart from evenings at the Victory, was first thing in the morning. He was an early bird and getting earlier by the year. The hour or two before Anna woke up was his own special time alone and undisturbed. Usually, he spent it in the front room reading one of the thrillers he devoured by the kilo. In the summer, if the weather was good, he would venture out onto the patio where he made himself comfortable on the sunbed. On occasion, he had been known to drift back to sleep until woken by Anna. But normally, the time was too precious to waste a minute.

He loved gardening almost as much as he loved the Eagles and crime stories. He devoted as much of the weekend as football would allow to weeding and pruning. Not for him the hard toil and meagre harvest of a crop of potatoes or scrawny tomatoes. Better to buy those at Aldi. His little kingdom was there to impress. At its centre a pond which, come summer, was a mass of Koi carp swimming under white and pink water lilies. Bill had to fight hard to protect the fish from raiding storks who thought nothing of downing a hundred-pound meal in one gulp. But that battle, despite the occasional casualty, was part of the enjoyment.

Despite the beauty of the pond, it was the beds and pots around it that made the garden for Bill. There was no denying the collection he had built up over the years was eye-catching.

Some might say a little too eye-catching. The foliage, though carefully curated, gave the impression it was completely unrestrained. Glossy fatsia leaves shaped like Martian's hands vied for breathing room with tree ferns, palms, and clumps of black bamboo that reached the height of the bedroom window. Lilies, fuchsias, and hibiscus provided colour while trailing passion fruit fronds added the finishing touch to the impression you were wandering through a primary school poster illustrating an imaginary rain forest.

It happened one Thursday morning in early June. The season was over. Palace had finished safely mid-table and it would be weeks before the start of their next campaign. For the past ten days, Bill had been reading a rather dull thriller about a Finnish detective who solved crimes using his sense of smell. Perhaps it lost something in translation. Or, perhaps, he didn't get Finnish humour. Whatever the reason, he was finding it less than compelling. In fact, he had already caught himself dosing off a couple of times when he saw a movement out of the corner of his eye.

He looked up. What he saw was more surprising than any twist of plot he could have anticipated in the novel. There, hovering by a white hibiscus bush, was a brightly coloured green and red bird about the length of his hand. Bill might have doubted what he was seeing but there was no question about it – the creature looked exactly like the one on the BBC documentary Anna had been watching the previous Sunday. *It's a hummingbird*, thought Bill as he sat and stared at the exotic visitor hanging in the air and jabbing its beak, backwards and forwards into one of the flowers. A couple of seconds later it darted away. Almost instantly, it was back repeating the jabbing in front of another flower.

A few stunned seconds later, Bill had collected his thoughts. Too old to be part of the generation that instantly captures anything unusual on their phones, Bill's instinct was to rush inside and share the experience with Anna. "After all," he reasoned, "if she enjoyed watching hummingbirds on TV, seeing one in real life would be even more exciting." Already thinking of the creature as Anna's Hummingbird, Bill edged quietly through the patio doors so as not to disturb the ongoing nectar collection and headed upstairs to the bedroom.

Anna didn't appreciate his attempts to rouse her. Without listening to what he was saying, she turned over and told him to leave her alone. Rebuffed, Bill headed back to his unexpected guest in the garden. It had gone. So had Bill's concentration. His attempt to finish off 'The Kokkola Mysteries' was futile. All he could think about was the hummingbird. Where had it come from? Why was it in his garden? But most of all, how could any creature be so beautiful?

For once, Bill couldn't wait for Anna to come downstairs. Over breakfast, he told her what he had seen. She was disbelieving. There were no wild hummingbirds in London. She didn't need a documentary to know that. But, thanks to David Attenborough, she could tell Bill they only lived in South America and the Caribbean. Tennison Road was a long way from either. They'd die of cold here. More likely Bill had dozed off and dreamt it.

The harder he tried to convince her, the more certain she became that he was imagining things. Bill knew he was defeated before he finished his cornflakes. He ate the last few mouthfuls in silence. Better to savour in his mind the blur of green wings than to tarnish the image by disputing it with a disbelieving spouse.

Walking to Norwood Junction and on the 08.08 all the way to London Bridge, Bill could think of nothing else. Why was such a creature flying around this part of South London? How did it survive? Would it come back? That question began to dominate his thoughts. Imagine if the hummingbird, or better still a pair of them, took up residence in his garden. That would be a step up from the Koi. There was no way anybody else in Norwood would have anything like it. Come to think about it, there was probably nobody in the country who would have anything like it. His garden would be truly unique. He could see television crews coming down to film it. His own fifteen minutes of fame.

Burning to share his excitement with somebody, but with no friends at work, Bill couldn't concentrate. The result was two mistakes, the first in five years.

It was still light when Bill got home. The first thing he did was to go out onto the patio. Examining every plant in the garden, Bill could find no sign of the bird that occupied his thoughts. Through a largely silent dinner, his mind was still in the garden and the rest of him returned to it as soon as he had finished his last mouthful. Bill stayed there, pretending to prune until, eventually, the descending dark forced him back inside.

He didn't stay long. The Victory and the chance to share his news with a sympathetic audience were too compelling. Leaving Anna in front of the TV, he headed out.

Not long after, with a pint of Guinness in his hand, Bill settled into one of the padded seats built into the bay window. Keith and Tom were already on their second pints. Bill was ready to tell them everything. He spoke to Keith and Tom more than to anybody else, always over a drink. Politics, football, other events of importance to South Norwood and even, on rare occasions, their families were the normal topics of conversation. Bill wasn't sure why it was so important to tell them about that morning's exotic visitor to SE25, but he had been burning to do it all day.

Things didn't go as he had imagined. Bill probably didn't know what reaction he wanted when he told them his news, but it wasn't, "Pull the other one, I never knew you were such a joker!". Once he had convinced his audience he was being serious, it only got worse. Soon everyone in the Victory was chipping in:

"Must be global warming."

"You should be more careful what you smoke mate!"

"I believe him, I had a pair of penguins on the roof the other day."

"Just as well you haven't got pixies. I hear they play havoc with lawns."

Bill soon left with his tail between his legs. That night, he couldn't sleep. He needed proof and he was going to get it. In the morning, he was up earlier than ever. Making no attempt to read, he sat, as still as possible on the sunbed, his camera, which usually only made an appearance for holidays, by his knee and surveyed the garden for any sign of movement. The white hibiscus was the focus of his attention but he glanced around the rest of his empire from time to time. He was convinced it was only a matter of time before he would see a flash of green and red and get the photo he needed. But, by breakfast time, he had had no luck.

That day, Bill changed his routine at work. Instead of working at a steady pace, he rushed and instead of stretching things out, he took shortcuts. As a result, by lunchtime, he was at the bottom of his to-do list. That left the afternoon free. He used it to research hummingbirds.

Bill spent his weekend on more (unsuccessful) bird spotting disguised as gardening. Anna did wonder about the camera constantly hanging from his neck, but she knew better than to say anything.

On Monday afternoon, Bill was back to his research after, once again, cramming his day's work into the first three and a half hours of it. Over the following days, the pattern repeated itself. Bill spent his entire day thinking about the hummingbird and his mornings and evenings looking for it. The rest of the time, he continued to learn as much as he could about them. He hardly slept. He didn't even go down to the Victory.

By the end of the week, Bill knew that there were 360 species of hummingbird and, in the process of trying to work out which he had seen, had learnt the names of almost half of them. He had eliminated a lot, some based on colour, others based on size, but he was still not sure what species he had seen. Although he had spent hours on it, identifying which kind of hummingbird he had seen wasn't Bill's primary concern. If he couldn't produce a photo, he wanted, at least, to prove to his sceptical audience that a hummingbird could survive in Norwood, that a hummingbird in his garden wasn't in the same category as pixies or penguins in Penge, and that, however unlikely, what he had seen was possible.

At first, Bill had researched other exotic animals that managed to survive in the UK. Wallabies, mink, and even

Mongolian gerbils managed but they were not terribly exciting and didn't really prove much. Yellow-tailed scorpions and escaped pythons were more exciting but not directly relevant and, in any case, it turned out that more often than not, the pythons died during the rigours of an English winter. The best he could come up with were a handful of Grey parrots and lots of parakeets. Nobody knew for sure how they came to be living wild in London, probably they were descendants of escaped pets, but there was no doubt that this Indian bird had established itself and was thriving in London. If they could do it, why not hummingbirds?

This took Bill back to hummingbirds and their habits. His discovery that they dined on insects and nectar was good news. There was plenty of both in his back garden. But, was England too cold for them? Anna was right, most come from the tropical parts of South America and the Caribbean. But not all. The Encyclopaedia Britannica said that hummingbirds were found right across the Americas from Tierra del Fuego to Alaska. That was interesting. If they could survive somewhere as cold as Alaska, then surely, London ought to be a doddle. A little more research told him that some now live as far north as Vancouver even in winter. Bill checked Vancouver's latitude. Only a hundred and fifty miles south of London and we have the Gulf Stream. That convinced Bill. He was sure a hummingbird could survive in London.

Armed with a headful of pertinent facts and figures, Bill was ready for another trip to the Victory. Once again, it didn't go exactly as planned. After a few minutes waiting for the conversation to come round to the subject naturally, Bill could wait no longer. He launched into a monologue on hummingbirds and their chances of survival in South London.

Eager to convince his friends that it was possible and he hadn't been imagining things, he transferred every drop of his new-found knowledge. He told them about the range of hummingbird's natural habitat, their eating habits and, most importantly, the way they can survive in subfreezing conditions by bringing their metabolism so low that they enter a state of torpor. A neutral observer would have seen that his friends weren't interested. But Bill was a man on a mission. He wasn't going to stop until they at least admitted it was possible he had seen a hummingbird. He ranted on, becoming increasingly passionate as he did.

Bored by what he had to say but amused by his performance, they egged him on. How long could a hummingbird survive when it was frozen? Did they eat bees? They kept the questions coming but were careful not to concede the possibility of a hummingbird in London. They insisted on the one thing he didn't have, hard evidence in the form of a photo.

As Bill's frustration rose, so did his volume. For the second time in a fortnight, he was the centre of attention at the Victory. Despite the passion Bill put into it and the science behind it, nobody was going to accept his argument. They continued to make the same simple demand, "Show us a photo, and we will believe you". In the end, the failure was too much for him to take. He stormed out and then spent an hour wandering around dark streets before going home.

After the performance he had given, nobody at the Victory was going to pass up the opportunity to tease Bill. Quite the opposite. From then on whenever he made a visit to the Victory, the first thing he would hear was, "How's the Hummingbird?", followed by, "Got any photos for us today?"

Then, inevitably, there followed a sequence of other, equally provocative, references to the bird he couldn't prove he had seen. Another man might have cracked, given in, and admitted it was possible he had imagined the whole thing. Not Bill. He had seen what he had seen and wasn't going to back down.

The standoff came to define him. It wasn't just that the regulars in the Victory were now as likely to refer to him as "Mr Hummingbird" as they were to call him "Bill", he felt a sense of betrayal. He had never really expected Anna to believe him. But, how could his mates be so disloyal? Watching Palace with them would never be quite what it had been and sharing a pint certainly wasn't. Nonetheless, Bill continued to do both. Even if his visits to the Victory, were not as frequent as they had been, he turned up often enough to demonstrate he was undefeated.

As time went on, Bill almost came to regret that chance encounter one Thursday morning. Almost but not quite. Even if nobody believed him, even if he was the butt of their jokes, he knew what he had seen. Those few moments were something special, something none of them had ever experienced.

Autumn

They Are Down There

Martin didn't consider it an obsession. Nobody who knew him agreed.

The few friends he had gave up on him one by one. Eventually, the only person willing to listen to anything he had to say about his Grand Theory was his girlfriend, Marie-Anne. Marie-Anne, in many ways, was the opposite of Martin. She had no interest in quirky facts, government cover-ups, or postulating about what was behind the news being served up to the public. For her, all that was outside her immediate world and, if she couldn't do anything about it, why worry? Why even think about it?

She stuck with Martin not because she believed his Grand Theory, but out of a sense of loyalty. Every time a friend walked away from him or made a disparaging remark about Martin's sanity, Marie-Anne felt she had to provide a little more support to compensate. This growing loyalty and a hope that, Martin would, eventually, abandon his obsession with the Grand Theory kept her going. So, of course, that night in February, when Martin announced Operation Deep Post, Marie-Anne, without hesitating, said, she was in.

She had been with him on more recces than she could remember. Not going on recces would have been incompatible with being his girlfriend. So, she put up with them. She even pretended to be interested in the places they went and what Martin had to say about them. He believed her. That was the important thing.

When Martin was still calling them walks, the recces were relatively mundane. True, some of the places they visited were a little odd. Not many people can say they have been in every catacomb in London – Highgate, West Norwood, Camden…the list is a long one. The Mithras Temple under the Bloomberg Building on Victoria Street had been more interesting and less spooky. Marie-Anne had genuinely enjoyed that. She couldn't say the same about the sewer visit. That was the low point. Then, once they got onto abandoned tube stations, things had picked up again. Some of those visits were exciting by anybody's standards. Throughout it all, Marie-Anne reminded herself it was a plus that they got plenty of exercise during the recces and, on most of them, a bit of fresh air. More than that, they were an opportunity to spend time with Martin.

Marie-Anne couldn't remember exactly when Martin stopped calling them walks and started calling them recces. Probably it was a gradual process. She did remember when he started to give their outings code names. The first was Operation Thespian. Marie-Anne had come into the living room and found a slim, red ring binder lying on the dining room table Martin used as a desk. Mildly curious, she had picked it up.

On the piece of card carefully pushed into the pocket on the spine of the file, Martin had written in his neatest handwriting "Operation Thespian" and on the next line, "Secret". Now Marie-Anne was genuinely curious. She knew

Martin wouldn't be back for another hour. So, she sat down and opened the file.

There wasn't much on the first page. But what there was stuck in her memory. A year and a half later, when the investigating officer asked, she was able to reproduce it in full:

Location Name:	The Old Vic Tunnels
Location Type:	Not-for-Profit Theatre, Railway Tunnels
Location Co-ordinates:	51.5022°N 0.1096°W
Primary Objectives:	1. Evidence of reason for closure 2. Evidence of T contact
Operation Date:	The last line was incomplete.

Eager to know more, Marie-Anne turned the page and continued to read the contents of the file. It was soon apparent Operation Thespian was not yet fully planned, but there was no doubt about the thoroughness with which Martin was going about it. Marie-Anne had always been impressed by Martin's powers of concentration and attention to detail. She was a big-picture person.

The file contained over fifty pages of articles, photos, and maps. Thumbing through them, she soon learnt that under Waterloo Station there was a maze of tunnels and other underground spaces that no longer formed part of London's transport system. A part of this labyrinth had been turned into a theatre and exhibition space. Quite a prestigious one it seemed, Banksy's film *"Exit Through the Gift Shop"* had premiered there. The file also contained a lot of information about the venue's finances, the high-profile people who had visited it and the layout of the tunnels that surrounded it.

The last sheet of paper was a list of questions:

Cover or target?
Who are the Old Vic Trustees?
Bloomberg connection?
Why close? No lack of funding. T contact?
Cameron's motives?
Clinton's role?
US-UK joint-operation?
Kevin Spacey/Kevin Fowler – military links?

Marie-Anne's feelings were mixed when she put the file down. She liked Martin's drive and focus; it showed an attractive mental strength. She didn't like the subject of his attention. What kind of hobby was this? Couldn't he channel his energies better? Could she do something about it? She didn't want to upset him, but surely, there was a way of getting him to do something more productive with his time. What was it? She hadn't answered her own question by the time Martin got home. She carefully avoided mentioning tunnels for the rest of the evening.

Martin's interest in the subterranean had started with, of all things, an article promoting a local pop-up bar. At the time, Martin was in his real ale phase. He had been an enthusiastic consumer of craft beer for almost a year. When he saw the article, he knew he had to go. Less enthusiastic and not a beer drinker, Marie-Anne agreed to accompany him on the basis that they went to her favourite Thai restaurant afterwards. "At least," she told herself. "This obsession with beer is better than when he spent all his evenings trying to set up an aviary in the loft."

The walk to the bar, located opposite the railway arches at the back of Elephant and Castle tube station, took less than five minutes from their home on Brook Drive. It changed their lives.

It wasn't the beers. There was no problem with them. It was their names. The brewery had decided to market its entire range using the "lost" rivers of London as a theme. As Martin sipped his pint of Neckinger, he asked the bar attendant not only about its specific gravity and the origin of the malt used in it but also the name. It turned out that Martin had picked a beer named after a river that flowed under Elephant and Castle.

Later that evening, back home, a Thai meal to the good, a slightly tipsy Martin googled the Neckinger. What he found fascinated him. The river really was local. More local than he imagined, he walked above it every day. It ran not just through Elephant and Castle but also under Brook Drive. The name of the street should have been a clue, but in the five years he had lived there, Martin hadn't once thought there might be an actual stream under it. Martin tried to imagine the river flowing below them, down to the Elephant and Castle roundabout, then parallel to the New Kent Road to Bermondsey and eventually St Saviours Dock. Who would have believed it? But, if Wikipedia said it was true, it must be.

He read more. The etymology of the river's name was one of those quirky details Martin's brain so loved. Apparently, in the seventeenth century, executioners used to hang pirates at the wharf where the river joined the Thames. The river got its name from the slang term for a noose, a "devil's neckcloth".

Martin's mind was whirring. The idea that there was a network of hidden rivers winding their way under the streets and buildings of London was intriguing. What were the other hidden rivers? Did they all have such colourful names? What bits of history were linked to them? He was going to find out. But not straight away. Marie-Anne, who was starting to get a little jealous of the Neckinger, dragged him off to bed.

Martin's interest in underground rivers turned out to be more than an alcohol-fuelled late-night fling. His imagination had been aroused. The next morning, he continued his research. And the next. And the next. He discovered the Earl's Sluice, the Effra, the Tyburn and the Wandle. He devoured all the information he could find about them and dragged Marie-Anne to an exhibition about them at the Museum of London Docklands. The Fleet, Lea, Walbrook, and Westbourne were added to his list. Martin was fast becoming an expert on London's buried rivers. He joined the Effra Redevelopment Agency and the Tyburn Angling Society. Later, when he realised their plan was to re-surface the rivers, he left. Martin liked the idea of secret underground rivers – if they were brought to the surface again, they would lose all their mystique. No, he yearned to visit them in their hidden underground tunnels. And it was possible. Martin discovered there were a surprising number of books containing guided walks along London's lost rivers. He ordered them all from Amazon.

The weekend after the books arrived, Martin and Marie-Anne went on their first walk. The destination was Silk

Stream. Marie-Anne had picked it when Martin asked her to choose one of the walks. The name conjured up exotic, decadent, and luxurious images in Marie-Anne's mind. Reality was a disappointment. As a river, the Silk Stream was nothing inspiring and the origin of its name, as she learnt when Martin read aloud from the book, was even more prosaic. It came from an Old English word meaning a plough or furrow. *So,* she thought, *this river is named after a muddy field!* Martin, who had in his haste, uncharacteristically done no planning other than buying the book, was disappointed for other reasons. He had naively assumed that every walk in each of the books would lead them through a series of underground passages. They didn't. Martin and Marie-Anne stayed at ground level for the entire duration of their expedition along the Silk Stream.

The setback only spurred Martin on. He doubled his research efforts and lowered his expectations. All their future walks were carefully planned. A couple of weekday evenings went into every weekend expedition. At first, Martin only managed to prepare for one or two walks a week. But, by using every evening of the week for research, Martin was able to fit three and eventually four walks into every weekend.

Later, Marie-Anne divided the evolution of their walks into three phases. During the first phase, Martin was only interested in underground rivers. They visited the Oval Cricket Ground to see the curve which follows a bend in the Effra and Deptford Wharf to see the Earl's Sluice arriving at the Thames. They even visited the infamous wharf at the mouth of the Neckinger. They were disappointed not to find any gibbets. For Marie-Anne, the best trip was the one to Hampstead Ponds. There they went swimming in one of the hidden rivers, or at least that is the way Martin put it, since Hampstead Ponds is where the Fleet disappears underground.

The sewers came near the end of the first phase. Martin had known for a long time that many of London's underground rivers had been turned into sewers. Sewers were accessible and so it struck him that getting into a sewer was probably his best chance to see one of his rivers underground. That's how Martin and Marie-Anne found themselves at Abbey Mills in Stretford one Saturday morning. As they stood in the pumphouse fully kitted out, she remembered thinking how impressive the building was and wondering why the Victorians had put so much effort into a sewage station. A few minutes later, the guide was leading them through the sewer below. The contrast could not have been greater. Even if the smell was not as bad as Marie-Anne had feared, she could think of nothing good to say about the place. Marie-Anne wanted to be supportive, but the next time Martin suggested a visit to a sewer, Marie-Anne told him to go alone.

He did. Well, not exactly alone – just without Marie-Anne. Over the next six months, Martin spent most of his free time making sewer visits with a group of like-minded enthusiasts. These visits were nothing like the Abbey Mills guided tour. They were unofficial forays. Finding hidden entrances, avoiding security cameras, and scrambling in and out of manholes became second nature to Martin.

Marie-Anne was pleased when the river phase transformed into the tube station phase. One Sunday in May, after Marie-Anne had hinted it would be nice to spend more time together, Martin said he would come up with something they could do together. When he suggested a trip to Sloane Square tube station, Marie-Anne wasn't exactly inspired but she jumped at the opportunity. It could have been so much worse. Saturday came and they set off.

The objective of the expedition was to see a pipe. Martin had read that the Westbourne flowed through Sloane Square station. He wanted to see for himself. In the end, although they found the pipe there wasn't much to it and neither Marie-Anne nor Martin found the visit that exciting. What did excite Martin was something he discovered during his preparatory research.

Over coffee the next morning, apropos to nothing, Martin suddenly said, "I can't understand it, why would you spend so much time and effort building them and then just abandon them?"

Marie-Anne was a few steps behind him. "Abandon what?" she asked.

"All those tube stations," Martin replied. Martin went on to tell her that he reckoned there were over a hundred tube stations in London that had been abandoned, partially abandoned, partially built but never completed or built but never opened. It just didn't make sense. The economic cost was huge. Martin wanted to know what was behind this waste of resources.

Instead of wading knee-high in sewage, Martin now wanted to visit tube stations or to be more precise tube stations that were no longer operating. Marie-Anne was all for it. After Sloane Square, the next tube station outings were two official London Underground tours of abandoned stations – Aldwych and Down Street. Marie-Anne found them remarkably interesting, something about the image of wartime Winston Churchill sitting deep underground in a bunker housed in a tube station she had never heard of, captured her imagination.

Having exhausted official tours of abandoned stations, Martin and Marie-Anne moved on to sites, the Old Vic Tunnels among them, that were still in use, just not as tube stations. Although a few of these locations afforded access to the tunnels, which were Martin's real interest, most of them did not. By Martin's reckoning, there were 14 deep site stations (surface stations he was happy to ignore) that had been operational at some point but were now completely abandoned. He wanted to visit them all. He set about it in his usual methodical and patient way. For each station on his list, he first researched the site and noted where the ticket hall had been. Then came an initial short recce. If the station buildings were still intact, it was an easy task to confirm the location. Even if the original building had been demolished or rebuilt, Martin found it was usually possible to confirm exactly where they had been from other clues. Now, armed with as much information as he could gather about the target site, Martin would work out the best way to gain access to whatever remained underground before, finally, putting the plan into action.

Even Marie-Anne was excited by the thrill of the first clandestine sortie. After a full briefing, Martin and Marie-Anne headed for the City. Using diversionary tactics to circumvent security, they sneaked into an office building just north of London Bridge. Once they were in, Martin led Marie-Anne down to the basement and, after a short search found a manhole in the floor. He opened it. Marie-Anne, despite the briefing, was taken aback by what she saw next. There, under the manhole cover, was a Victorian cast iron spiral staircase. At the bottom of the stairs, Martin and Marie-Anne found themselves on the platform of King William Street tube station. It was a moment of triumph.

Their visits to the remaining stations on Martin's list were almost as exciting. His preferred modus operandi involved hiding in the closest station until two am. Then, after it closed scrambling along the tracks, torch in hand, to the forgotten neighbour. Every recce set the adrenalin running and there was a strange sense of awe inspired by the dirty platforms and the things they found on them. Holding a sixty-year-old ticket or a similarly aged shoe in her hands (why would anybody leave a shoe in a tube station?) sent a little thrill through Marie-Anne.

Eight months after the tube station phase started, Martin was still working through his list and Marie-Anne was still accompanying him on every expedition. She felt much closer to him now than she had during the sewer phase, so she was surprised she had no inkling of his Grand Theory until he announced it fully formed.

Marie-Anne had invited her friends, Jen and Paul, around for dinner. They were among the dwindling number who still accepted invitations from the couple. The sewer phase had taken its toll. It wasn't so much the faint aroma that always surrounded Martin, more the fact that all he ever talked about were those pungent underground waterways. Jen and Paul had stayed strong. Marie-Anne, they reckoned, needed their support. So, when they arrived, they were ready for yet more sewer stories. When instead Martin started to talk about the British Museum station, it was a pleasant surprise.

First came a few historical facts. The station opened in 1900 with its entrance on High Holborn. It closed in 1933. The official reason for the closure was changes in plans for the line. Martin went on to explain that he believed the real reason was more sinister. In the years before the closure, large numbers of passengers reported seeing people dressed in nothing but loincloths, moving around the tunnels and making strange noises. A rumour spread that a mummy had escaped from the British Museum and was running around in the tunnels under it.

"And you believe that?" asked Paul.

"Of course not," said Martin somewhat peevishly, "if you hang on a minute, I'll tell you what I do believe." He went on to explain that after the British Museum station was closed, sightings of the same strange figures were reported at the next station along the line, Holborn. Most people at the time dismissed the sittings as the figments of imaginative minds. But that wasn't possible after what happened in 1935.

Martin paused. He was clearly playing his audience, Jen took the cue, "What happened in 1935?"

"Two women disappeared from one of the Holborn platforms," Martin went on, "the only clues left behind were some unexplained scratch marks. For the next few years, strange noises were heard from behind the tunnel walls and the 'mummy' was sighted again several times. That creature is the real reason for the closure of the British Museum station," concluded Martin.

"So, if it wasn't a mummy," asked Jen, now hooked by Martin's story, "what was it?"

"Well, of course, the whole mummy story was a smoke screen to divert attention from what was really going on. The truth is, it was a Troglodyte." Martin was met with confused stares. "A person who lives underground," he explained.

"What, some sort of tramp who found the tube a warm place to shelter?" asked Paul.

"No," said Martin, "a person who was born and has lived all their lives underground. Part of a community that has existed under London for centuries."

This needed an explanation. So, Martin outlined his Grand Theory. He believed the person seen in the Holborn tunnels (and it may have been different people at different times) was a descendant of a tribe that had lived in the area since before the Romans. When Caesar's armies arrived, this tribe, probably after some initial skirmishes, had understood they could not beat the Romans. Rather than being wiped out, or surrendering, they decided to go underground both metaphorically and literally. Living in caves and a network of tunnels that they gradually expanded, they kept themselves out of harm's way, only emerging at night to forage and steal. It was a waiting game. When their time came, they would return to the surface once again and claim victory.

Unfortunately for them, throughout the Roman occupation, the Troglodytes' time never came. The Roman's trump card was their superior technology. From the beginning, the Troglodytes were one step behind. It stayed that way. The conditions they lived in didn't favour the advancement of science, so they could never catch up with the Surface Dwellers. The Surface Dwellers would invent a technology and the Troglodytes would steal it during one of the night raids but by then the Surface Dwellers were onto something new. Despite this, the status quo persisted. Out of sight and out of mind, the Troglodytes were safe in their underground labyrinth. For as long as they were successful in keeping the entrances to their underground safehold secret, they could go undetected. Even if the Surface Dwellers had breached the entrances, and perhaps they did on occasions over the centuries, the Troglodytes' superior knowledge of their subterranean environment and the narrow passages would have given them an advantage. Like the Greeks at Thermopylae, a small band of Troglodytes could hold off a vast army of Surface Dwellers for days. The Americans faced much the same in Vietnam where the troops they were fighting made up for inferior weapons by using an extensive network of tunnels. "Remember," said Martin, "the Vietnamese came out on top."

Over the last two millennia, the evidence suggested encounters between the Surface Dwellers and Troglodytes had been relatively rare. The hidden tribe had no desire to be discovered and the Surface Dwellers were blissfully unaware of what lay beneath their feet. But, as the population of Surface Dwellers in London had increased, contact had become more frequent. There were several accounts of what must have been Troglodytes captured by Surface Dwellers during the eighteenth century. Then during the late nineteenth century and early part of the twentieth century, the Surface Dwellers started to dig sewers, underground railways and tunnels for their gas, water, and telephone lines to pass through. Contact became more common. Incidents such as the Holborn Incident were covered up by the government as best possible. They didn't want to frighten the population by revealing the danger below them. Most of the abandoned underground stations are on the deepest lines. That's where all the encounters took place. That's where the Troglodytes have their base.

All of Martin's incredulous listeners had questions. Marie-Ann, not wanting to seem unsupportive, kept hers to herself. Jen and Paul were more forthcoming. "How could the Troglodytes survive for so long underground?"

"Easy," replied Martin, "They aren't the only people around the globe to have lived underground. The classical world has hundreds of examples, Herodotus, Aristotle. and Diodorus all wrote about them." Seeing he hadn't yet convinced anybody, Martin went on. Did Jen and Paul know about Petra and Vardzia? Or, more pertinently, had they heard of the city of Derinkuyu in Anatolia? They had to admit they hadn't. Derinkuyu dated from nearly four hundred years before the London Troglodytes founded their subterranean home. And it's not the only underground city in the area, more than two hundred of them exist and they are all linked to each other by a network of tunnels. Even though Derinkuyu itself fell out of use in 1923, others are still being used. Like the home of the London Troglodytes, Derinkuyu was a place of refuge. Who built it originally and who they were hiding from is still not clear. But there is plenty of evidence that over the centuries, Derinkuyu and the other cities have been used by the local people to hide from wave after wave of invaders. The Arabs, Abbasids, Mongolians, and Ottomans all pillaged and tried to subjugate the local people, but safe in their underground cities the locals outlasted them all.

To give his audience some idea of the scale of what might be right under their feet, Martin went on to explain that Derinkuyu is located nearly eighty meters underground comprised of hundreds of miles of tunnels and is eighteen stories in depth. In all, there is room for 20,000 people and their livestock to live there. Livestock is crucial. Cows and sheep can survive underground with limited visits to the surface and, if forced to, people with the right genetic makeup, as the Maasai show, can perfectly well live off nothing more than blood, milk, and meat. The diets of Troglodytes everywhere must be similar (although, of course, supplemented by whatever they can gather during foraging raids to the surface). Diodorus, for example, described his Troglodytes living off cattle in exactly this way.

The others had nothing to say.

That point settled, Martin went on to put forward another piece of evidence pointing to the existence of an ancient city and network of tunnels under London. It was a mosquito. Not any ordinary mosquito, a specially adapted mosquito. In overground London, mosquitoes are like those in other cities and towns around the world. They mostly feed off birds, hibernate in winter, and require a lot of space and stagnant water to reproduce. In the tunnels and passages under London, mosquitoes are different. Just after the end of World War II, scientists discovered what they named the London Underground Mosquito. This is completely different to the aboveground version and perfectly adapted to the conditions in which it lives. It doesn't hibernate in winter, can reproduce in close proximity, and has a propensity to live off human blood. It would take hundreds of years for such a creature to evolve from the normal British mosquito. Quod probat, a subterranean London with human inhabitants must have existed for hundreds of years otherwise such a mosquito would not have been able to evolve. Martin postulated that these mosquitoes had probably escaped from the Troglodytes' city into the London tube system around the time of the Holborn Incident.

And why did the Troglodytes abduct two women? That was obvious. Even without a knowledge of genetics, societies around the world have understood since prehistory that to stay healthy, there must be a constant renewal of blood within small communities. The illnesses and deformities that inbreeding causes are eventually fatal. Societies around the world have come up with many different solutions to the problem but bride kidnapping is one of the most popular. People have resorted to this on every inhabited continent, even Europe. Think of the Sabine.

His Grand Theory proven, Martin stopped.

There was a long awkward silence. Marie-Anne saw Jen and Paul looking at each other as if to ask, "Is he being serious, or is this a joke?" Not knowing, they said nothing. Marie-Anne, sensing danger in continuing the conversation, changed the subject. Later that evening as she said goodbye to Jen and Paul, she knew they would not be back. Martin's eccentricity had gone too far. Although it hadn't been the boring evening they feared, somehow, hearing the way he talked about his Grand Theory, they were no longer comfortable around him.

It wasn't long after Jen and Paul's visit that the military phase started. It was sparked by Martin's discovery that the owner of almost all the abandoned tube stations he had been studying was the Ministry of Defence. "Why," he asked, "would the Ministry of Defence buy up disused tube stations?" It only made sense if the stations were contact points with hostile or potentially hostile Troglodytes. That would be a good reason for putting them under the army's supervision and keeping them as military facilities until they were fully secured and confirmed as safe.

In addition to the stations and tunnels, Martin discovered an extensive list of other military assets hidden under London. His files on Q-Whitehall, Pindar and the other installations were as comprehensive as any civilian files could be. The facility that initially interested him most was the so-called Cabinet War Rooms. These were the oldest of the underground facilities built by the government and it was the timing of their construction that intrigued Martin. Work on them started in 1938. Given the slowness with which Whitehall operates, that probably meant the project had been conceived two or three years earlier at a time when nobody foresaw the war with Germany. Martin ruled out the possibility that Stanley Baldwin, an arch-appeaser, had the vision or desire to prepare for a war he was confident he could avoid.

Perhaps the 1.2-hectare facility had originally been intended for another purpose. Perhaps it was no coincidence that the project must have kicked off at about the same time as the Holborn Incident. That view seemed to be borne out by the engineering facts. The facility had been created by strengthening an existing basement. Strangely, the underground walls and floor offered more protection than the ceiling, which official sources confirmed was vulnerable to a bomb strike. If the construction was supposed to protect the prime minister from Hitler's Luftwaffe, why build it to a design that meant it could be taken out by a single well-directed bomb? No, if you wanted to protect it from the air, you would build it like the Admiralty Citadel, just down the road, which was constructed a couple of years later with a reinforced concrete roof more than six metres thick. That was an authentic Word War II facility.

If the Cabinet War Rooms were in fact not built as a bomb shelter, then what were they built for? Martin's conclusion was that the whole complex must have been built in response to the Holborn Incident or others like it. The true purpose of the facility must have been to protect Whitehall from a potential subterranean attack. That also explained the other thing that troubled Martin – the secrecy that surrounded the Cabinet War Rooms. Whilst there had been absolutely no attempt to disguise the fact that the Admiralty Citadel was being built, the existence of the "Cabinet War Rooms" was not made public until 1984 despite officially being decommissioned shortly after the War.

Martin was certain they must have had an ongoing military role pretty much all the way up to 1984. Of course, if the government was worried about an attack from under their feet, the first thing to protect would be the capital's centre of military and political power and the last thing that they would want would be for the public to know anything about it. Could you imagine the panic? From that point of view, the story about the facility being Churchill's wartime command centre was a useful piece of misdirection and opening it as a tourist attraction an absolute masterstroke designed to firmly imbed the official version of the truth in the public mind.

Operation Deep Post took place on a Thursday night in February. It was only the second nighttime recce Marie-Anne had been on with Martin.

The target was Kingsway. Marie-Anne knew from Martin's briefing that officially the facility had been built under Chancery Lane tube station in the early 1940s as a deep-level air raid shelter. It had been extended in the 1950s by the addition of extra tunnels. The government admitted it had never been used for this purpose. Instead, according to their version of events, it had been converted into an archive for public records and then used as a telephone exchange before being decommissioned in the 1980s.

Martin scoffed at the idea anyone would build a sixty-metre deep, twelve-mile network of fully air-conditioned reinforced concrete tunnels with their own generators and the capacity to house 200 people and then use it to store old files. That made no sense. A more rational explanation wasn't hard to find. On the map he was using for the briefing, Martin pointed out that Chancery Lane was one stop along the Central Line from Holborn, which in turn had been one stop from the British Museum station. His working theory was that there had been an initial fatal and fateful encounter between the Troglodytes and the Surface Dwellers at the British Museum station. The station had been closed and sealed off. Following the incident at Holborn, the army had worked out that the Troglodytes had got into the British Museum station from Holborn and that their main base was somewhere even further east. Kingsway was dug as an exploratory tunnel with the objective of confirming the exact location. Once confirmed, the army turned Kingsway into a monitoring post. The equipment that had been stored in the tunnels wasn't a telephone exchange, it was sophisticated listening equipment used to spy on the Troglodytes.

The objective of Operation Deep Post was to get into the Kingsway facility and learn as much as possible about its true purpose. Originally, there had been three ways into Kingsway. One, off Tooks Court, had been demolished. The second was next to a shop front at 32 High Holborn. But it was the third, on Furnival Street, that they were going to use.

Martin outlined his plan and concluded the briefing with a list of emergency protocols.

Marie-Anne and Martin left Brook Drive at midnight. An hour later they were approaching Furnival Street from the south, they walked arm in arm, like any other couple on their way home from a night out, much as they had that night when Martin first discovered the Neckinger. The road was a mix of modern and older buildings. Some looked as if they might be private homes others were clearly offices. They stopped outside No. 10. Later Marie-Anne could remember every detail of the stone columns and ornate skylight over the door. Shivering a little in the cold, they pretended to kiss while Martin surveyed what lay ahead.

The target was in sight, No. 39 a few metres away on the other side of the road. It looked like an ordinary building except for the lack of windows on its first two stories and the fact that it was the dirtiest on the street. Martin stared at the two black doors and quickly glanced each way down the street. All clear. Pulling his hoody over his eyes, he went up to the smaller of the two doors. As he did, Marie-Anne noticed a red sign on it reading "Fire Exit Do Not Obstruct". Martin did something to the door. It opened. Marie-Anne, her hoody also in place, ran across the street and joined him. They were in.

Kingsway was nothing like Marie-Anne had imagined. For a start, it wasn't dark. No need for torches. The whole complex was lit with fluorescent lights. And it was clean, at least cleaner than she expected. There was none of the dust and debris she had got so used to on other recces. It was also warm, which was a relief after the cold outside. She had noticed the underground tunnels they visited were always cooler in summer and warmer in winter than the surface. But Kingsway seemed unusually warm.

They started to explore. Marie-Anne was fascinated by how extensive the facilities were. It wasn't all equipment. There were sleeping quarters, toilets with running water, a canteen and kitchen, a room that looked as if it had been set up for playing snooker and even a bar. Martin paid little attention to the living facilities, he was more interested in the equipment and the layout of the facility.

Martin had been very clear during the briefing that they should stick together throughout the recce but, about an hour after they started their exploration, they found themselves separated. Martin had gone ahead, Marie-Anne had stayed behind poking around in a cupboard in the kitchen but was now on her way to rejoin him. Suddenly, she saw Martin running down the corridor towards her. "Get out!" he shouted.

Marie-Anne started to run too. As she turned away from Martin, she saw, out of the corner of her eye, a figure chasing after him. Sprinting as fast as he could, Marie-Anne tried to remember what Martin had said during the briefing. Now she wished she had paid more attention. With adrenalin doing its thing and her legs moving as fast as they could, it was hard to recall. When were they supposed to run and when were they supposed to surrender? Suddenly, she slipped on something greasy on the floor and was on her knees. A second later, she was back on her feet. As she set off again, it came to her - it depended on who the "hostile" was and whether they were armed. If it was an armed Surface Dweller, they would surrender, get a slap on the wrist and that would be it. Better that than getting shot. If it was an unarmed Surface Dweller, they would leg it, trying to escape wouldn't make any punishment worse. If it was a Troglodyte, there would be no way to communicate. So, they would run anyway. As Martin was running, whoever was chasing them must either be an unarmed Surface Dweller or a Troglodyte. How did it help to know that? *Why*, thought Marie-Ann, *am I wasting time thinking about why we are running, what's important is what we do next.*

Behind Marie-Anne, the two sets of footsteps seemed to be getting closer. She was almost at the staircase. Then there were a couple of bangs, a muffled shout, and silence. Marie-Anne thought about turning round. Better not. The instructions were everyone for themselves. She carried on and was soon bounding up the steps as fast as she could take them.

Fifteen minutes later, panting but physically unharmed, apart from a gash on her left knee, Marie-Anne walked into the local café where Martin said they should meet if they got separated. She might be okay, physically but she was a mental wreck. What was she supposed to do now? What was the protocol? She tried to remember what Martin had said during the meeting. She was supposed to call him. She tried. No answer.

Half an hour and five failed calls later, Martin had still not joined Marie-Anne. She called the police. They arrived surprisingly fast. After taking down all the details Marie-Anne could give them, they suggested Martin might be at their home. They drove her there. There was no sign of Martin. Telling Marie-Anne to call them if Martin turned up, the police left.

Later that day, the police were back. They asked a lot more questions. Where did his parents live? Did he have any brothers or sisters? Where did they live? Who was his closest friend? Did he often go off by himself? Was he on any medications? Taking a photo of Martin with them, they left again.

The next time they came, the police asked for Martin's toothbrush. It seemed a strange request. It wasn't reassuring when they explained they needed the toothbrush to get a sample of his DNA.

The third time they came, the police searched the whole flat and asked Marie-Anne a lot of questions about Operation Deep Post. How long had Martin been planning it? Where had he got his information? How had he known the way to get in? Marie-Anne didn't know the answers. This time the police left with Martin's computer and all his files.

In the months that followed the police made no progress. They didn't find Martin and, what was worse, they didn't have any idea where he might be. How could he disappear so completely? Marie-Anne went over events in her head again and again. The police said they had searched the whole Kingsway facility. If he wasn't there, he must have been caught and taken somewhere. So, who caught him? Who was it chasing him in the tunnel? A security guard? A Troglodyte? Or somebody altogether different? How could the police be so incompetent? Perhaps they weren't. Were they just covering something up? Was Martin's Grand Theory true?

Marie-Anne never did get the answers she was after.

Judgement Day

Ashley woke at six thirty and immediately knew it was Judgement Day. He had been dreading it all week. To be more accurate, he had mostly been dreading it. Some small part of him had, in a masochistic way, had been looking forward to it. Now all that mattered was that it was here. There was nothing more he could do about it. Resigned to the inevitable, he started his usual Sunday routine. It hadn't changed for seven years – wake, go out for a run, shower, down a carefully calibrated breakfast and then head off to the gym.

Reading this, you might think Ashley had always been something of an athlete. You couldn't be more wrong. As a child, he had never had any interest in sport. He'd always enjoyed reading more than running and food more than friends. Perhaps "friends" isn't the right word to use in this context. Although he called them that, most people would have referred to them as his classmates and neighbours. Although he wished it was different, he wasn't close to any of them. Not least, because they never stopped teasing him. There was always some way to make fun of him. His bookishness, his stammer, but most often, his weight offered opportunities that were eagerly grabbed.

Weight was a problem. Ashley had been chubby for as long as he could remember. The sedentary life he lived with his mother's connivance, was more than a little to blame. That and his eating habits.

Ashley's father had died in a car crash when he was one. So, the family budget was entirely dependent on what his mother could earn from her writing. She was a good journalist and for her, freelancing from home worked well. She took whatever assignments she could get whether it was for the Sunday Times or an obscure trade rag. She always delivered on time and her pieces never needed editing. It was no surprise she quickly established a stable of editors who relied on her.

Her diligence meant that, even when rates were not good, she somehow managed to balance the books. That achievement came at a price – time. She had none of it. She was constantly researching or writing. Spending time with Ashley was fitted in around work. Only one ritual was sacred – story time. This was Ashley's favourite part of the day. For those few minutes each day, he basked in his mother's undivided attention as she read to him and finally tucked him into bed before going back to her work.

His mother believed it was those bedtime stories that first encouraged Ashley to read. Whether or not she was right, there was no doubt he was a motivated learner. When most of his peers were still struggling with the alphabet, he was already reading books. For his mother, it was a godsend. If she ever needed some quiet time to make a phone call or finish an article, she would give Ashley a new book and a bag of crisps confident in the knowledge that he would be quietly absorbed for as long as it took her to complete her task.

It was just after his seventh birthday that the doctors first suggested it might be a good idea for Ashley to lose a bit of weight. They suggested more exercise and some adjustments to his diet. Ashley's mother did her best to comply. From then on, they ate a lot more salads and carrot sticks replaced crisps as Ashley's reading snack.

Getting him to exercise was harder. The list of failures grew by the month. His mother's first attempt was to send him to ballroom dancing classes. It would be a gentle introduction, she thought, and the children looked so cute fox trotting around the room. It was a disaster. Ashley hated it. More than anything, this was because it provided yet more ammunition for those who enjoyed teasing him.

He suggested that he do something a bit more manly. Playing for Arsenal had always seemed like a good career path, so it didn't take much to persuade Ashley to join the Camden Elite Under 9 team. The adventure didn't last long. After the coach made it clear that Ashley was never going to be more than second reserve right back and shouldn't aspire to an appearance more than every other match, his mother had to agree with Ashley that he was unlikely to ever become a professional footballer. If that wasn't going to happen, Ashley didn't see the point in going to practice anymore and didn't.

Karate was a little more successful. Kai, the trainer who led the group, liked Ashley's mother and sympathised with her efforts to get Ashley active. He took a special interest in the novice. Ashley responded well. Naturally disciplined, he wanted to please Kai, who was only the second person he remembered ever showing any interest in him. During class, Ashley listened attentively to every word Sensei uttered and copied his actions as closely as he could. At home, his mother was pleased to hear him shouting, "Ichi, ni, san, shi…" as he practised kata in his room.

Ashley sailed through his red belt. Yellow he passed with little difficulty and orange wasn't much harder. Green followed, after a struggle, but as much as he wanted to, Sensei couldn't convince himself that Ashley's performance deserved purple. Stuck at green, while the rest of his dojo progressed through the remainder of the rainbow to black, Ashley lost interest. He practised less and less and eventually dropped out.

No future sporting venture was as successful. During his teenage years, Ashley started something and gave up another dozen times. He showed no aptitude or enthusiasm for any of them. Although he would have liked to lose a bit of weight and believed he would have more friends if he were thin, Ashley never believed it was in his power to change anything.

Ashley's academic progress was better. Whilst not a genius, he was clearly of well above average IQ and his teachers loved not only his aptitude but also his diligent attitude. His ability to concentrate was the talk of the staffroom. Still without any real friends or interests, but finding encouragement from his teachers, Ashley concentrated on his studies. Good GCSEs led to A Levels and a place on an information and library studies course at Aberystwyth University. After graduating, he fell into a job as the assistant librarian in a large legal firm in the City.

He settled into a routine of commuting to work, eating TV dinners when he got home, and indulging his passion for reading at the weekends. He had ballooned during his years at university, where quite remarkably he had managed to be even less active than he had been at school. It made squeezing his 1.85-metre, 140-kilo body into a crowded tube carriage every morning and evening a bit of a pain. The comments from other passengers, some openly expressed, others whispered to neighbours, made painful listening. Apart from that, Ashley felt his life wasn't too bad.

Everything changed with the layoff. Somebody at work had the bright idea of reviewing efficiency within the firm. One of the conclusions was that two librarians were one too many. The severance package was generous, but it didn't compensate for the feeling of being unwanted. More than that, it reinforced Ashley's sense that life was beyond his control. He moved back in with Mum.

That Christmas, Ashley's Aunt Liz was visiting. Although he had only met her a handful of times, Ashley found her fascinating. He didn't quite understand what she did for a living, and it seemed rude to ask too many direct questions, but it meant living abroad and seemed to involve moving from country to country every few years. Most people would have described Aunt Liz as eccentric. It came across in both the way she dressed and the way she behaved. But for Ashley, the most important thing about Aunt Liz was her unrelenting positivity. She was always smiling and encouraging those around her, and she would never acknowledge the word failure existed. Ashley remembered a previous visit when she had cajoled him into persisting with one of his doomed sporting endeavours. It had worked, while she was around and for a few weeks after, but in the end, the inevitable had happened. Ashley had forgotten long ago which sport was involved but he still relished the memory of being encouraged in such an enthusiastic manner.

Sensing that this time Ashley was on the point of giving up not just on sport but on his whole life, Aunt Liz swung into action. On Christmas morning, her present to Ashley turned out to be a red envelope covered in gold stars. Ashley thought it must be money. He was secretly pleased – he could do with the cash. When he opened the envelope, the contents were a disappointment. No fifty-pound note, not even a twenty, or a ten, just a small hand-made voucher that announced his aunt had bought him three sessions with a celebrity life coach. Ashley would have struggled to hide his disappointment if Aunt Liz hadn't spoken so energetically about the vision and wisdom of this amazing person and what he had done for so many of her friends. "Go and see him," she said, "you will thank me later!"

Ashley did go to see the life guru, not because he had any belief in the outcome, but simply to please his aunt.

As he arrived for the first session, Ashley had a sense of déjà vu. The whole thing had the feel of taking up yet another new sport. Three sessions later Ashley was thinking differently. Now, he was placing everything he encountered into one of two categories – things outside his "sphere of influence" and things inside it. Only the latter mattered. Anything in the former was tolerated but ignored. The way Ashley spoke had also changed. Anybody prepared to listen to him for more than five minutes soon learned that the keys to success are proactivity and willpower. They then got a lecture about understanding, having a clear vision, prioritising and taking time to "sharpen the saw". Finally, there on the corkboard above his bed was a small postcard declaring his new philosophy:

*"God, grant me the serenity to accept the things
I cannot change,
Courage to change the things I can,
And wisdom to know the difference."*

The new Ashley set himself two missions: he was going to find a great new job and he was going to lose weight. Despite setbacks, he persisted with both missions. The easier of the two turned out to be the job. Several hundred applications and three months later, Ashley was Chief Librarian at another City firm. He acknowledged that the title was a little grand given he was the only librarian there, but what of it? The job was exactly what he wanted.

Losing weight didn't come so easily. He reduced his calorie consumption and started to take walks every day (running at that time was beyond him). Gradually, he increased the distance he covered. Progress was slow. But it was measurable. Once a week, he would weigh himself and record how many grams he had lost. As the months went by, his fitness improved. As his fitness improved, the distances he covered increased. With both, his weight continued to recede.

After many months, running became a possibility. One summer morning, instead of walking his normal route, Ashley decided to jog a shorter one. It was a partial success. Halfway round, out of breath and with his body feeling like lead, he couldn't run anymore. He completed the course at a walk. But, nonetheless, it was still a victory. He had run halfway round the course that day, the next day he would run more than half and eventually, he would be able to do the whole thing. His weight loss chart was developing a parabolic curve.

Seven years on, Ashley was still in the same job and still working on his weight. It had only taken him a couple of weeks to get to the point where he could make it round the whole of that first short course at a slow jog. After that achievement, Ashley slowly increased the distances and speeds he attempted. Every run and every weigh-in was logged and analysed. Every month he set himself new targets for distances, pace and weight loss. Every target he hit brought a sense of achievement and a desire to achieve yet more. After a few years, he was covering distances and running at speeds none of his colleagues at work could match.

There had been setbacks, of course. Every time he went on holiday, he came back a little less fit and a little bit slower. A couple of bouts of flu had the same effect. The time he had to rest a stress fracture for six months was both physical and mental torture. But he had persisted and progressed. The key was his analysis. He looked at every aspect of his training. What was in his sphere of influence and what was not? What could he control and what could he not? Could he change the pattern of his runs? Take up another sport as a form of cross-training? Tweak his diet? Cut out a bad eating habit? Working out what he could do and then doing it was satisfying.

What had been less satisfying recently were the results. The shape his weight-loss graph had developed worried him. Over the years, a steep upward slope showing the kilos he had lost had been the reward for his initial efforts. Then the graph started to flat line. At first, the adjustments he made helped him maintain upward progress. But now it was getting harder and harder. The line had become almost horizontal. Struggle as he might, he was no longer looking at kilos but, once again, measuring progress in mere grams per month. Worse than that, he was running out of options for improvement. Holidays had already been eliminated, calorie consumption could not be reduced much further, and increasing distances would only increase the risk of another stress fracture.

All of this was going through Ashley's mind as he pounded out his morning run that Sunday. It was still at the centre of his thoughts as he stripped off and walked into the bathroom. As he did so, he glanced sideways at his body in the mirror. It didn't look good. Still far too fat. He pinched his skin to check. Yes, there was still room for improvement. The immediacy of empirical judgement pushed the question of how to achieve that improvement to the back of Ashley's mind. It was time. As much as it scarred him, he had to know the result.

Ashley pressed his right foot down on the scales firmly but did not commit his entire weight. A light flashed on, and a row of zeros appeared in the display panel. Ashley knew that if he did nothing the light would flicker out in ten seconds. The moment had come. Ashley slowly lifted his right foot once again and placed it gently on the scales. As he did so, he resisted the temptation to look down. Now the left foot. This was the trickiest part of the whole operation. One jerky movement, a little bit too much pressure and the reading would be distorted. Ashley's left foot joined his right. Time to look down.

56.1 kg.

No progress. The week had been a failure. Ashley resolved to try harder before the next Judgement Day. Perhaps if he ate only every other day…

Moving On

It was a Saturday morning when Jade finally cut her losses and left. In many ways, she was sorry to be leaving. It was the best flat she had ever had. It had been a dream living there. If the dream could have gone on, that would have been great. But Jade had known for a while that this time would come. She had to leave. If she hadn't been through the same thing before, Jade might have stayed a little longer. A little too long. Like the first time. There was no way she was going to put herself through that again. Being evicted wasn't a pleasant memory. The angry words, the bailiffs, but most of all the humiliation were all seared into her memory. There was no way she was going to allow that to happen again.

Along with the regret, Jade did feel more than some small sense of relief as she closed the front door behind her for the last time. It was over. As wonderful as the flat was, the last few months had been difficult. Very difficult.

How different everything had been when she moved in. Referencing, which could have been tricky, had gone without a hitch. Jade had scraped together enough to pay the deposit and a month's rent in advance and the landlord, Mr Wilson, who had insisted on being there when she turned the key in the lock for the very first time, had been all smiles and charm as he flirted with her. Jade, who enjoyed the attention almost as much as the new flat, had to admit she had egged him on a little. She had told him all about her modelling career and all the amazing places she had been on photo shoots. She had even shown him a few pictures from her portfolio. She could feel him succumbing. He didn't put up a fight. She would soon have him around her little finger, just as she wanted. Not a bad thing to have the landlord under her control. She just had to be a little careful. She wasn't the only one wanting something out of the relationship and what Mr Wilson wanted wasn't just the rent. As if anything like that was ever going to happen! But there was no harm in letting him have his dreams.

To be fair to him, despite the drooling, Mr Wilson had been the perfect landlord for the first few months. He fixed the shower within a day of Jade's asking. He came round to change a light bulb when she told him it was on the blink. He had ogled a bit when Jade answered the door in her dressing gown, but she had planned that, and his eyes had been quick to focus back on hers. *Yes*, Jade thought, *although he had lingered a little too long chatting and smiling, he had kept everything just the right side of the line.*

When Jade failed to pay the second month's rent, Gary, as he had asked her to call him, was exceptionally good about it. Nobody had noticed the payment hadn't gone through until a couple of weeks after it was due. Then with the exchange of messages between her and the agency, it was almost the end of the second month before things were settled. Jade explained that finding money for the deposit and a month's rent in advance had been difficult. Her previous landlord had not yet returned her deposit. Gary said he understood and, because she was "such a nice young woman", he had agreed to her suggestion that she settle the arrears when the deposit was finally returned. Would Gary have been so accommodating if she looked like a dog? Jade wasn't sure. Perhaps he had a kind heart. Did it matter? Not really, they had reached an agreement that suited her and that was the important thing.

Jade had been aware of just how much power her good looks and strong personality gave her for as long as she could remember. At primary school, she had always landed the big parts in school plays. No third donkey for her in the nativity. From her very first performance, Jade had made sure she was centre stage. Somehow deep inside her, she knew that was where she belonged. She had something her classmate didn't. She was special.

Waiting for the performance to start that dark December evening, Jade had, for the first and only time in her life been nervous, very nervous. But, when the curtain went up and she was suddenly the focus of the universe, her nerves evaporated. There had never been a purer or more loving Mary. You sensed a halo over her head as she trudged towards Bethlehem and glowing divinity as she cradled and cared for the baby Jesus.

Jade's first adrenaline high lasted well after the last member of the audience stopped clapping at the end of the performance. Whatever concerns Jade had before the show were gone forever. Jade knew there was no audience she couldn't handle. All she wanted now was to get back on stage once again.

At secondary school, while her friends got their buzzes however they could, Jade stuck to acting. She knew it was an addiction, but she was hooked. It wasn't just the exhilaration of sucking all that energy out of the audience. Jade also loved the opportunity acting gave her to leave the rest of her life behind. Living, even for an hour or two, in a world where the extraordinary came true beat Enfield hands down.

Money meant that drama school was never an option for Jade. So, she had made it her mission to find an agent that would take her on straight from school. Being Jade, she, of course, succeeded. A few parts in professional performances followed. But, even for a talented actress, and nobody doubted Jade's talent, there were times between. It was during these times that modelling became a part of Jade's life. Her rare combination of acting ability and good looks helped her pick up the occasional modelling assignment. She took to it. The kick she got from the clicking of the shutters and knowing how many people would be looking at the result was almost as good as the one she got from the clapping of audiences.

When Jade missed another month's rent, Gary was once again surprisingly sympathetic. He suggested he should come round to discuss the problem. "These things," he said, "were always better dealt with face to face." *Any excuse!* Jade thought. But she agreed, no point upsetting him.

This time, Jade opened the door wearing an all-leather outfit consisting of knee-length boots, a mid-thigh skirt, and a half-zipped jacket. The expression on Gary's face confirmed, as Jade had expected, that he liked the look on her. Settling into a bucket chair opposite Gary, Jade told him she was wearing the outfit because she had to leave for a shoot in a quarter of an hour. She sensed disappointment. A month's rent was a lot to pay for fifteen minutes of pleasure.

She decided to give him his money's worth. Crossing and uncrossing her legs a little more than was strictly necessary,

Jade told Gary that her previous landlord had still not returned the deposit. Then she explained that in her line of work, cash flows were unpredictable. Everyone thought models were rolling in it. But it was only a lucky few. For everyone else, it was harder. When Jade was working, the money was great, but when she wasn't...With the disruption of moving, she hadn't been able to fit in as much work as she would have liked. She had even had to turn down a job in New York. But luckily, the money for the fashion shoot she was about to do was good. When she got paid, Jade would settle everything. As Jade bundled him out of the door, Gary, who was clearly thinking about her thighs rather than the rent, agreed she could have the extra time.

The more time she spent with him, the more Gary reminded Jade of Mr Taylor, her Year 10 maths teacher. There was something so familiar about the covert glances up her skirt and the quick look in another direction when he thought Jade was about to notice. When she had first noticed Mr Taylor's interest in her, Jade hadn't been quite sure how to react. On the one hand, it was all a bit creepy. On the other, his attention gave Jade the same thrill she felt on stage or in front of a camera. More, even. She sensed her power to control him was far greater than that she exercised over even the most pliable audience. He accepted any excuse she made up for not handing in her homework. It soon became a habit. Despite that, her marks improved.

Best of all, Mr Taylor was the first male adult that had ever shown any interest in Jade. Jade couldn't remember her biological father. Her mother called him a charming con artist. He had walked out of their lives when she was three, so Jade couldn't say if that was true, but she did wish he was still around. Mr Taylor's interest wasn't exactly fatherly but Jade thought she could make a kind of substitute dad out of him. It was nice having a bit of attention. Even nicer having that much power over another person. So, Jade did what she needed to keep him interested (the leg crossing trick dated from the Mr Taylor era) but never went too far. For his part, Mr Taylor was either too clever or too scared to do anything more than look and be nice. The whole thing was over by the start of Year 11.

A few weeks after the leg-crossing display for Gary, Jade was unlucky enough to have to tell the letting agent, that she was never going to get the money for the shoot she had been on. Unfortunately, she explained, the company that had hired her went bust before paying. In the meantime, a massive tax bill had arrived. She would have to defer paying the rent once again. Luckily, she was expecting another large payment from an advertising shoot she had done in Paris a couple of months ago. When it arrived, she would have no problem paying the arrears.

It was around that time that Gary's charm started to evaporate. The sweet tone and puppy dog looks were gone and his next visit to the flat was far more business-like. The irritation in his eyes was clear as he told Jade she couldn't defer the rent again. Jade sat patiently through his rant. But complain as much as he liked, she knew there was nothing he could do. He had to accept the situation. If Jade couldn't pay, she couldn't pay.

At the end of the next month, things got even worse. By then Mr Wilson, as he now insisted on being called, seemed to have lost all interest in direct communication with Jade. So, Jade found herself explaining to the letting agent that she still could not pay what she owed. There had been some problem with the payment. There always was when things came from abroad. She did everything she could to smooth things over. She once again promised to pay the arrears as soon as she got the money she was owed. But right now, it was just not possible. What could she do? She wasn't a banker, and her cards were maxed out. They would all just have to wait for the payment to come through.

The agent showed no sympathy.

Jade started to get official demands to pay.

Over the next couple of months, the agents continued to chase. Jade continued to make the best promises she could.

When Mr Wilson got involved again, Jade knew things were getting serious. He started to call her every other day. If she answered, he would give her a piece of his mouth. She stopped answering. He started to visit. On the first occasion, Jade repeated everything she had already told the agency. She couldn't pay right now but she would as soon as she could. Shaking with anger and virtually screaming at her, Mr Wilson was forthcoming about what he thought of Jade and her non-payment. Jade was a little frightened.

The next time Mr Wilson came round, Jade pretended to be out.

Then there was the Sunday morning confrontation. Jade was on her way to pick up her usual eleven o'clock latte at Costas. As she walked out of the building, there he was, right in front of her, not more than a metre away. Their eyes met. She could see he was about to explode once again. Before he could, Jade smiled and said, "Gary, nice to see you! I was going to call. I have some good news. I've been paid. I'll send you the back rent tomorrow." That seemed to calm him. After muttering something inaudible, he turned and left. Jade grinned and went to get her latte. That was the last time they saw each other.

The agents never received the promised payment.

It was only a week or so later that a brown envelope with a fancy crest arrived at the flat. The letter inside was addressed to Jade Ballard. She was being taken to court for the arrears. Jade did nothing. What could she do?

The first brown envelope was followed a month later by another containing a judgement.

When the enforcement order arrived, Jade knew things were nearing the end. She had lost this battle. But she was a survivor. She would find another place to live.

It only took a couple of days.

So, as she walked out of the lift into the lobby, she knew she had a place to go to. Jade thought about handing her key to one of the concierges as she walked past their desk. But she decided not to. She hadn't liked Gary from the beginning, and the way the lech had handled things towards the end had done nothing to improve Jade's opinion of the pathetic loser. No, she would quietly drop the key into a gutter or throw it off a bridge. That was it – let him look for it at the bottom of the Thames!

Now, she was on her way, Jade was excited about the prospect of moving into her new flat. Nine Elms, right next to the American Embassy. That was a step up from Canary Wharf. She was proud of herself for arranging everything so quickly and efficiently. The new place was going to be even better than the one she was leaving. It ought to be, the rent was twice what she had been paying Gary (or if you wanted to be pedantic, hadn't been paying). But then, private cinemas and a glass swimming pool a hundred meters above the ground don't come cheap.

Jade looked at her watch. She had better hurry. When she had done the viewing, the furniture in the new place hadn't really been up to standard and she had told the agent to get rid of it. She was expecting a delivery from Mariner that afternoon. She wanted to be there when they arrived.

Of course, when the agent for the new place called the mobile number Jade had given him to get a reference from Mr Wilson things could have gone badly. To be honest, Jade was surprised that he did call. Based on her previous experience, Jade knew most agents couldn't be bothered to take up references. Never mind, it had gone well. Mrs Wilson confirmed that Jade had made all her rental payments on time and on top of that, couldn't help mentioning what a terribly sweet, clean, and considerate tenant she had been.

Despite never expecting to have to play it, the role had been one of Jade's best. She had performed it perfectly. It had been so exhilarating. Jade could do anything she wanted! She was a genius. Not just as an actress. Her photoshopping was also brilliant. No one had raised a single question about her forged payslips and doctored bank statements.

Now she was going to enjoy the fruits of her labour. The first month, before she even had to think about excuses for not paying, was always the best. She was going to enjoy the gym and spend as much time as she could in the pool. It was going to be special looking down through the transparent floor at all the little people below. It was good to be moving on!

Winter

A Miscalculation

It was Monday morning. Adam got onto his new bike and set off for the City and work. He stuck to the route he had planned so carefully over the weekend, following back streets and cycle routes wherever possible. If he had calculated things right, the journey would take no longer than the tube. In his head, he started to go through the maths once again.

"No," Adam told himself. "Concentrate on what you are doing. Stay focused!"

That was good advice, given this was Adam's first experience of negotiating the hazards of London's streets on a bike. He had learned to cycle in the safety of a small park near his parent's home but, until now, had never been brave enough to go out on the roads. The thought of negotiating the multiple hazards in store for him was more than a little daunting. Adam was correspondingly nervous. But he egged himself on. It was going to be worth it. The experience couldn't be worse than the tube!

Despite his lack of confidence, the first part of Adam's journey went as well as cycling through rush hour London in pouring rain could ever be expected to go. Off the back streets, he headed down Holloway Road and onto Liverpool Road. There was one incident when a pedestrian had unexpectedly stepped out in front of him. Fortunately, nobody was hurt and overall, Adam was feeling good about things. Just past Angel tube station, he turned onto the A501A. As he approached the Old Street roundabout, Adam told himself how well he had coped. Even better, it looked as if his calculations had been too conservative. Travelling by bike was going to be faster than taking the tube. This was a triumph, not only was he getting exercise as he travelled to work, but there was also a certain macho pleasure to be had from the whole process. He had managed to brave the elements and the challenges thrown at him by the other road users, he was in control!

Perhaps Adam shouldn't have attempted to wipe his glasses as he cycled round the roundabout. If he hadn't, he might have seen the white transit van sooner. If he had, he might have avoided it. As it was, Adam didn't notice the van until it turned sharply left, cutting in front of him and making a collision inevitable.

As the paramedics carried Adam's unconscious body to the ambulance, the police started to compile their report. There wasn't much in their description of Adam to set him apart from a million other men in London. White, of South European appearance, his hair was dark brown and curly, and they noted, as we already have, Adam wore glasses. Other than that, Adam's face had no particular distinguishing features. He was slightly overweight (but not the only man in London who fell into that category) and of average height - too short to stand out in a crowd but too tall to be the last into a rush hour tube carriage without having to bend his back and neck to fit the curve of the door.

That is exactly what he had done every weekday morning for the six months before that fateful day. You could say it was his choice. No one had forced him to move to Lidyard Road. Before, when he used to travel from High Barnet, he always managed to get a seat. But, from Archway, it was a different story. In those seven stops, rush hour trains filled to capacity, which meant standing all the way.

Adam hadn't factored that into his calculations when he decided to move. What he had focused on was the shorter journey. From Sedbright Road, it never took less than fifty minutes to get to work. From the new place, it would take half an hour. Those twenty minutes each way added up to two hundred minutes a week or (allowing for holidays) nine thousand six hundred minutes a year. That was one hundred and sixty hours, very nearly a whole week. It was the thought of all the things he could do with the extra time that had finally persuaded Adam to make the move.

Adam knew he needed to lose a few pounds and planned to spend exactly half his saved time every Sunday doing something about it. From Lidyard Road, he could walk to Hampstead Heath in twenty minutes, spend another hour walking round it and twenty minutes coming home. Adam couldn't imagine a better way of getting the exercise he needed. He had never been one for sport. It wasn't just his flat feet or the thick glasses he needed to see anything further away than the back of his hand. Somehow, it had just never appealed. On the other hand, some of his best memories were of Sunday afternoon walks on the Heath.

Adam's parents had always kept sacred the tradition of Sunday lunch followed by a walk. Every week, except in the most extreme weather, Adam, his brothers, and sister were dragged out of the house. They always complained loudly. At least, until they reached the Heath. Then they would run and shout, enjoying the freedom of space for that one short hour.

Six months after the move to Lidyard Road, Adam was still not sure if he had done the right thing. His life was now at once both better and worse than it had been. On the plus side, his outings to the Heath were the high point of his week. The downside was his journey into work.

True, Adam spent less time travelling than before. But he had come to realise that the quality of his travel experience was at least as important as its duration. You couldn't say he had enjoyed the daily trip from High Barnet. Quite the opposite. Adam was somebody who valued his personal space. He loathed every minute he had to spend cooped up in a claustrophobic carriage with sneezing strangers giving off aromas that ranged from the mildly unpleasant to undoubtedly obnoxious. The saving grace had been that he was always able to sit with his eyes focused on his phone screen intently ignoring everybody around him as the train got fuller and fuller.

From Archway, there was no way to do the same. Even if it was a good day and he was able to grab a bobble spring or piece of metalwork with one hand and extract his phone from his pocket with the other, he was constantly jostled and distracted as people pushed past him. On a bad day – and most were bad – he spent the entire journey with his arms pinned to his chest, his back arched against the door behind him and his neck cricked forward as he struggled to stay on his feet every time the train accelerated or lurched to a halt.

It was a very bad Friday that changed everything for Adam. Rushing to make the train, he was the last through the doors before they edged shut, nudging him forward and forcing him into the semi-embryonic position he was now used to assuming. As usual, his face was millimetres away from the head of the person in front of him. Although he had no way of determining the gender of the head, he was well placed to admire its glossy black hair and appreciate the strong scent of coconut that wafted from it. Adam closed his eyes and tried to imagine himself on the Heath.

When the train eventually arrived at Moorgate and ejected him onto the platform, Adam opened his eyes. His vision was blurred. He blinked a couple of times, trying to bring the crowd around him back into focus. It didn't work. Adam took his glasses off his nose and peered at them. It was only then he understood the problem. An indeterminate, semi-opaque substance covered the entire surface of both lenses with greasy streaks. As Adam tried to see more clearly what the substance was, the same smell of coconut he had been inhaling for the past fifteen minutes reached his nostrils. With it came the revelation that his loss of sight was caused by a thin layer of hair gel from the sleek head that had been his travelling companion all the way from Archway.

Holding his glasses with the tips of his fingers, Adam negotiated his way out of the station in a half-blind state. As soon as he arrived at his office, Adam disappeared into the toilet and, using a large quantity of paper towels, gingerly removed the hair gel from his glasses. In that instant, Adam decided that he was never going to travel on a rush hour tube again.

That evening, Adam took a black cab home. The next morning, he was the first customer to walk through the doors of his local bike shop. When he walked out, Adam had everything he needed. He was going to cycle to work on Monday.

Chloe

There was no doubt that Chloe was an aristocrat.

If you bothered about that kind of thing, you could trace her lineage back more than thirty generations, each ancestor as distinguished as the previous. All had names the length of a short novel and many had stories of success or heroic failure to go with them. She had inherited their classical good looks – an imperial nose and long, dark hair were her most eye-catching features.

Daddy was somebody important in the City. Mummy, although she was a St Andrews History of Art graduate, had never had a job. Keeping an immaculate home and arranging long-talked-about dinner parties for her husband's friends and colleagues was work enough.

Although she was born on a country estate near Cupar, Chloe had come to live with her family in London when she was only a few months old. Most of her life had been spent in a very comfortable five-bedroom, three-storey-plus-basement home in Chelsea with a more than adequate back garden.

Despite the size of the house, there were just three of them who lived there. Four if you counted Maria, the maid. For Chloe, the one who mattered most was Daddy. Daddy was the centre of her life. She craved his attention above all else and was only truly happy when he was playing with her or patting her on the head. Somehow, the way he did it and the way he called her his princess, made her feel very special and loved. Despite her overwhelming affection for Daddy, there was still space in Chloe's heart for both Mummy and Maria. Maria especially. Maria was, after all, the person who fed and looked after Chloe. More than that, Chloe spent most of her time with Maria and enjoyed it all whether it was taking a walk along the Embankment or simply watching Maria do chores around the house.

But that was all in the past.

Sometimes, Chloe found it hard to grasp that she was now living in Battersea and alone. Alone that is if you ignored all her noisy neighbours, and Chloe tried to do that as best she could. Growing up, she would never have imagined it was possible to crowd quite so many residents into such a small space. There must have been more than a hundred of them living in that one building.

Mummy and Daddy might be just a mile or so away on the other side of the river but the divide between them was irreparably deep. On her walks with Maria, Chloe had often looked across to Battersea but, until she moved there, she had never ventured south of the river. She had certainly never considered living on the wrong side of the water. Her relocation only came after a complete breakdown in her relationship with Mummy and Daddy.

For a while, when she was very young, Chloe had been the focal point of the household. Mummy was delighted to have her. In her eyes, there was nothing Chloe could do wrong. She was cute and cuddly, and any small mishaps were quickly forgiven. Daddy also evidently loved her. Even after a long day in the office, he would spend hours playing with her. She lapped up the love he gave her.

But as Chloe approached adolescence, something changed. Mummy and Daddy somehow seemed more distant and less interested in her. Mummy never spoke to her. Daddy was now always too tired to play after work. Maria was the only one left with time for Chloe, but she was paid for that.

Chloe knew something was changing. She tried harder and harder to get Mummy and Daddy to give her the same attention they had previously lavished on her. Nothing seemed to work. All her little tricks just annoyed them. She never understood that by persisting, she was only making it worse. Gradually, the stunts she pulled got more and more extreme and the rift wider and wider. One day, she even gave Daddy a gentle nip on the hand, pressing her teeth just deep enough to make an indentation but not enough to break the skin. This wasn't done out of any desire to hurt, just to show him she was there and needed him. He took the injury well but didn't love her any better for what she had done.

Things came to a head with a single incident. It turned the slow slide in Chloe's relationship with Mummy and Daddy into a rapid terminal descent. That night, in the dog days of late July, it was hot and oppressive. Maria had gone to visit relatives and Mummy and Daddy were out at a party. Chloe was home alone all evening for the first time.

Whether it was boredom, an anxiety attack, or simply a rush of freedom to the head, no one but Chloe will ever know. Whatever the reason, it is fair to say she went a little mad. She decided to have her own party and let herself go wild.

It was just after midnight that Mummy and Daddy walked through the front door. Seconds later, the carnage Chloe had created was evident. The floor of the hall was covered in debris – mangled flowers, shredded cushion stuffing, and a large puddle of what looked like water. Mummy might have been able to stomach all of this. What tipped her over the edge were the shards of blue and white porcelain that confirmed her favourite Ming vase was now an unsolvable 3D jigsaw puzzle.

When Mummy and Daddy arrived in the sitting room, Chloe was lying asleep in the middle of the carpet, the remains of a cushion under her head. She woke as they came into the room and, perhaps forgetting what had happened earlier that evening, bounded up to them full of joy. But there were to be no cuddles. That was quickly obvious. Chloe had never seen such a look of rage on Mummy's face. Then came the wildly swinging hand that hit the side of Chloe's head as Mummy shouted, "You little bitch! How could you?" Whimpering, Chloe ran into the kitchen to hide from the attack.

Daddy, although no less angry than Mummy, stayed calmer and eventually managed to calm Mummy, too. Neither ever spoke to Chloe again. That night she was kept locked in the small utility room in the basement and the next day, she was kicked out of the house. Despite their anger, Mummy and Daddy showed some pity and didn't leave her on the streets. Maria was given the task of finding Chloe a new home. Battersea was the result. It was also Maria, who eventually drove her the short distance to where she now lived. Maria was silent all the way and didn't say a word as she left Chloe for the last time. But, if Chloe had looked, she might have just noticed a small tear that almost appeared in one of Maria's eyes.

Chloe's new home was not a happy one. If she had been a bit down during her last days in Chelsea, she was miserable in Battersea. No friends, no family, not even Maria for company. Chloe succumbed to depression. She slept badly. Her looks faded. She longed for Daddy and one of his trademark pats on the head and hoped she would soon see his face. But he never appeared. Lethargic and out of sorts, Chloe oscillated between ignoring and barking at those visitors who did bother to come to see her. Needless to say, they never stayed long and never returned. Soon there were none.

This state of affairs went on for months, getting worse day by day. Chloe felt trapped, caged in and abandoned. The only thing she wanted was to escape from her prison in Battersea back to her once happy home in Chelsea. Her dream never came true. As Chloe lay down for her last night in captivity, resting her chin on her front paws, she had no idea that morning was going to bring one final visit to the vet, an injection and then, at last, release.

Border Dispute

It wasn't the kind of thing that normally happened in Richmond.

So, when it did, it inevitably drew the attention of all the neighbours. Well, it wasn't so much the event itself that drew their attention, most of them missed that, it was more the sirens of the police cars and ambulance immediately after. The occupants of the first car to arrive moved quickly. One of them ran to the figure on the pavement and started to administer first aid. His colleague went to the woman kneeling on the kerb and, crouching next to her, put her arm around the woman's shoulder.

As the first officer tried to resuscitate the unconscious man, the second spoke to the crying woman who she had now gently pulled to one side. "What's your name dear?"

"Amy," came the indistinct reply.

"I'm Jen," said the police officer. "So, Amy, is anyone else hurt?"

"No," said Amy. "I don't think so."

"And is that your husband?" Jen asked, looking across at the man with the blood-stained shirt.

"Yes, that's him," confirmed Amy with another big sob.

"Don't worry, Mike's looking after him, the ambulance will be here soon. They'll fix him up," said Jen. "While we are waiting, can you tell me what happened?"

"He was stabbed," said Amy.

"Yes, can you tell me a little bit more about how it happened? Who stabbed him? Did you see where the attacker went?"

"It was Barry," came the reply.

"Who's Barry?"

"He's our neighbour at 179."

"And where is he now? Did you see where he went?"

"Oh, he went home as soon as he had done it," answered Amy.

"Did he take the knife with him?" Amy nodded.

Turning away for a moment, Jen spoke to two more police officers who had just pulled up in a second car. "Confirmed knifing," she said, "the suspected perpetrator was seen going into number 179. His name's Barry, he lives there, and he probably still has the knife."

The two new arrivals went straight to the door of 179 and knocked. There was no answer at first. "Police. Please open this door!" one of them shouted.

Jen had now turned back to Amy. "Shall we go into your place?" she asked.

"Oh, I can't do that, I can't leave Jim," replied Amy.

"Look," said Jen pointing to an ambulance that was now parked a couple of meters away, "the paramedics have arrived. Better to leave things to them and not get in their way." Amy, who couldn't think clearly about anything just at that moment, let herself be led to her front door. While Amy was fumbling with her keys, Jen looked across at Mike, who had now moved out of the way to let the paramedics deal with Jim. Mike caught Jen's eyes and shook his head.

By the time Barry came to his front door, Amy, accompanied by Jen, had disappeared through hers. The conversation between Barry and the two police officers in front of him was short. A few seconds later, he was in handcuffs and being led towards one of the four police cars now parked along the road. One of the police officers accompanying him was carrying a plastic bag containing what looked like a kitchen knife. The small huddle of curious neighbours and passersby that had gathered, was held back as Barry went past but he could still see the bewildered expressions of surprise on their faces.

As Barry was placed into the back of the car, one of the neighbours was explaining what had happened to the others. "I saw it all," she said, "Jim came out of his place looking like he was going to explode. It was so not like him, and I couldn't understand why he had a knife in his hand. Amy tried to stop him but she couldn't. He rushed over to Barry and Mary's and started hammering on their door. He put the knife up to Barry's chin and they spoke for a bit. I couldn't hear what they were saying. The double-glazing is really good. Then Barry just grabbed the knife and stabbed him. That's when Amy started screaming. I called the police. I'm surprised how quickly they got here."

Inside 177, Amy had nearly finished making a pot of tea. Almost as soon as they got inside, Jen and Amy decided it was the best thing to do. Amy was happy to do anything to stop herself from thinking about what was going on outside and Jen was able to use the time to call her colleagues. The news wasn't good. But she was going to have to break it to

Amy. Jen waited until Amy had poured the tea and they had both sat down at the kitchen table.

Jen had always thought breaking the news of a death to relatives was the worst part of her job. Despite her training, she never quite knew how to do it. Today was no exception. In the end, she just blurted it out, "I'm sorry Amy, I have some bad news for you. Your husband has passed on."

At first, Amy didn't take it in. "You mean he is at the hospital?"

Jen was blunt, "No, I am afraid he is dead."

Amy said nothing.

All she could do was sit in her chair and stare straight in front of her. She couldn't even cry anymore. Then she began, almost under her breath, to utter one word repeatedly, "No, no, no…"

Jen did what she could to calm and comfort Amy. She told her to let her feelings out, made another pot of tea and asked if Amy wanted her to call anybody. Amy did. So, Jen called Amy's best friend, Lucy, who said she would be there in half an hour. "Do you want me to stay with you until Lucy gets here?" asked Jen. Amy nodded.

"You don't have to if you don't want to," said Jen, "we can always do it another time, but, if you want to, you could tell me the rest of what happened this morning?" Amy somehow sensed that talking might be therapeutic, that's what she was going to do when Lucy got there. She could tell Lucy how she felt or, at least, talk to Lucy and find out how she felt inside the numbness that now enveloped her. But, in the meantime, telling the policewoman in front of her how it all unfolded might somehow keep her mind off the way it all ended up. Amy nodded.

"So," said Jen, taking out a pen and notebook, "tell me how it started."

"It was after breakfast," said Amy, "Jim went out to do some work in the garden. When he got out there, he saw what Barry had done and he went ballistic."

"What had Barry done?" asked Jen.

"He had tipped a load of rubbish into our garden. When I say a load, I mean a load, it must have been the contents of five or six black bin bags. He must have been saving it up for a while. There were eggshells, bones, bottles, plastic containers, and bits of rotting food all along that side of the garden. When he saw it, Jim came into the kitchen picked up my fish-filleting knife and went straight out of the door. I tried to stop him, but I couldn't. Nobody can stop Jim when he gets like that," Amy paused for half a second and then corrected herself. "...got like that." Another pause, then Amy continued, "You see Jim is that type. He doesn't normally confront anybody but believes in things being done right. When somebody doesn't play by the rules, he gets furious. If he sees somebody drop a crisp bag on the pavement, he'll tell them to pick it up. He did that once and nearly got punched for his efforts."

"After Jim went out what did he do next?" asked Jen, bringing the discussion back to the morning's events.

"He went round to the Turners."

"Turner, that's Barry's family name. Right?" Jen checked.

"Yes," said Amy.

"And then?"

"Then Jim started hammering on the door. When Barry came out, Jim gave him a piece of his mind. I thought that was going to be the end of it. But then Barry said, 'If you can't be bothered to keep your fence in good nick, why do you mind about a little bit of rubbish in your garden?' That tipped Jim over the edge. He put the knife up to Jim's throat and said, 'If you pull a trick like that again, I'll use this on you.' Barry didn't say anything more. He just grabbed the knife and used it on Jim. Then he calmly walked back into the house and closed the door. I can't believe it."

After another minute of silence, Jen asked another question, "That thing Barry said about the fence, what was that all about?"

"Well, when we bumped into the Turners in Sainsbury's on Saturday morning, the whole thing kicked up a notch, Jim told Barry what he thought of Barry getting a solicitor involved. Jim doesn't usually do it, but he used some pretty choice language. I don't think Barry liked it, especially Jim airing our dirty linen in public. The rubbish must have been his revenge."

"I'm still not sure I get it," said Jen. "What's the solicitor thing about? And what does it have to do with the fence?"

"The fence on the Turner's side of the garden is our responsibility," explained Amy. "It got into pretty bad shape over the years. About two months ago, Jim decided it was finally time to do something about it. He likes that kind of thing. Liked that kind of thing. So, he was going to do it himself. He'd even ordered everything he needed. Then, a day or two before it was due to be delivered, Barry came round here and lectured us about the fence. He told us that the gaps in the fence were ruining the look of his garden. That it was our responsibility to maintain the fence and that he expected Jim to get it fixed within a month." Amy paused. Then she went on, "Jim's a good man…was a good man." She corrected herself again. "Normally, he was kind and gentle and wouldn't do anything to harm anybody. But, like I said, he didn't like it when he thought somebody wasn't doing things the way they should. That's when his stubborn streak came out. He didn't like anybody telling him what to do at the best of times. This time, it was Barry's tone more than anything else, especially when Jim was planning to mend the fence anyway. Jim didn't think Barry should have talked that way. Especially not to us, before this all started, we were such good friends. Used to get together every Saturday. If Barry had just said things nicely. Anyway, as soon as Barry left, Jim cancelled the delivery and refused to do anything about the fence. That was the end of Saturday evenings together. Jim wouldn't even speak to Barry. But Barry wouldn't leave it alone. He kept on about the fence, popping little notes through our letterbox almost every day and those notes got ruder and ruder. Then, about two weeks ago the solicitor's letter arrived."

"So, what was in the solicitor's letter?" asked Jen.

"It threatened legal action if we didn't mend the fence. I'm never going to be able to look at that fence again," sobbed Amy. After a few seconds of silence broken only by Amy's sniffing, Jen saw, through the tears, a new look in Amy's eyes before Amy finished her sentence, "And I'm never getting it mended."

Spring

One Day in the Life of Maria Popescu

As usual, at six o'clock the alarm clock went off sounding as loud as a hammer hitting a metal rail. Maria's hand reached out from under the blanket, without thought, stretching towards the offending noise.

The beeping ceased.

Her eyes half open, Maria looked through the bedroom window. Living on the eighth floor and not being overlooked, she never drew the curtains. That way, she could stare out of the window whenever she wanted. The window, or rather the view from it, was the best thing about the flat. She loved seeing London spread out in front of her as if she owned it all.

As Maria's eyes focused on the scene outside, she saw that everything was just as it had been in the middle of the night. There was no moon and no sun. If it wasn't for the light emanating from the buildings and streetlights, everything outside would have been pitch black.

Maria usually jumped out of bed as soon as the alarm rang. Today she did not. She had felt a bit feverish the night before. The hot lemon and honey concoction she had taken seemed to have helped but she still didn't feel 100%. Perhaps she was coming down with the flu. There was a lot of it about and she always caught it. She just couldn't cope with London's particular variety of cold. Somehow, in this damp and windy climate, it crept through your clothes and got into your bones however many layers you put on. She thought of Braşov. It could be cold there too, colder than London, but somehow the cold didn't cheat. If it was five degrees, it felt like five degrees, not like minus five.

Maria didn't get up. She lay there, her head buried under the duvet until the very last minute she calculated it possible without being late for work. Then she slipped out from under the covers and headed to the bathroom.

Twenty minutes later, Maria was heading out of the building to be greeted by yet another overcast sky. Why was there never any sun in this country? Maria thought back to her childhood summers. Every year her parents, wanting some time to themselves, had sent her out of Braşov to stay with her grandmother. Maria never really missed them. There was too much to enjoy in her grandmother's village. Maria loved the freedom and space. That and the undivided attention of a grandmother who somehow managed to scold and spoil Maria all at the same time.

Maria needed nothing more than the thought of those wonderful days to keep her spirits up all the way to school. Her memories were lemon-tinted. She remembered the bright yellow of ripe lemons hanging on the trees next to her grandmother's home and the duller green of half-ripe lemons. She remembered the baskets of collected fruit in the shed, the kitchen, and even the room where Maria slept. Maria remembered the distinctive aroma of the slowly shrivelling rinds her grandmother left in the fridge to keep it smelling fresh and the feel on her hands of the lemon juice and salt mix her grandmother insisted she use when cleaning dishes. Maria also remembered the same juice going into the water her grandmother used to cook rice. When Maria asked, her grandmother explained that she added this special, secret ingredient to keep the rice light and fluffy. Now Maria did the same herself.

Maria arrived just in time for the start of *'Breakfast Club'*. There was nothing in her contract that forced her into school that early, but it meant a little extra money and it wasn't that demanding. Maria rather liked the opportunity to interact with the children outside the classroom and there was something satisfying about knowing you were making sure they got a good, healthy meal.

As the start of lessons approached, Maria braced herself. She would have to face Oliver, her nemesis, the class clown who consistently tried to provoke Maria with rapid-fire wisecracks calculated to disrupt. Maria admired his cleverness but wished it could be better directed. It hadn't taken long for Maria to realise that the primary motivator of Oliver's outbursts was a craving for attention. Her response, following the advice of one of the old lags amongst her colleagues, was pre-emptive. Feeding his need before he started to misbehave, she always made sure she talked to him about something he enjoyed when he arrived in class. Then, during the lesson, Maria directed a disproportionate number of questions to him. These were all ones she expected Oliver to know, but nonetheless, she lavished praise on him when he answered them correctly. It was tiring and even though the tactic was good, the results were sometimes mixed. Today it worked. No more than a couple of uninvited utterances came out of Oliver's mouth. He made excellent progress with the maths problems Maria gave him.

Morning break was probably the low point of Maria's day. It started with a discussion about internet speeds. Somebody in the staff room complained about how slow their broadband was. This led to a more general conversation about remote working. Maria, uncharacteristically, had ventured the opinion that Romania was the perfect place for digital nomads. It was cheap to live, there were some fantastic tax breaks for IT workers and plenty of great things to do when you were not working.

Maria regretted it immediately. *'Vorba e de argint, tăcerea e de aur.'*

The looks on her colleagues' faces told her none of them could imagine her home country was a place anybody would want to move to. Maria sensed, one or two, Jack in particular, thought her a hypocrite to say what she had. If it was so good in Romania, why was she over here? Did she have to tell them she was a maths teacher, not an IT worker?

Nobody said anything. Janice, clearly feeling awkward, broke the silence, "I'm sure it's a lovely place for a holiday but to work there, wouldn't you need proper internet access?" Piqued, Maria pointed out, a little too sharply that, with the sole exception of Monaco, Romania had the fastest broadband service in Europe. The conversation ended.

Maria was used to this type of exchange in the staffroom. Things being said without being said. In the entire time she had been teaching, Maria had never been the target of any openly disparaging or discriminatory remarks. That would not have been politically correct, and all the other teachers knew it. After all, their jobs depended on knowing what was and what was not. More than that, almost without exception, they would have described themselves as open-minded and liberal. They might occasionally poke fun at some of the policies the Trust came up with, but they genuinely believed in the ethos it promoted. That somehow made it worse. At least if somebody was being openly offensive it was easy to challenge them. Perhaps she should have asked Janice why she assumed Romania had poor internet. But that would have been even worse than snapping at her. After all, she hadn't deliberately set out to provoke. With her colleagues, Maria knew anything they said to upset her was entirely without conscious malice. It simply came from some deep routed sense of superiority. It was almost as if knowing they were on the side of the angels, her colleagues felt they lived on a plane above other people.

Maria went back to classes. She felt frustrated and dirtied by the experience. *Forget them, make your own happiness,* she thought to herself. But she still couldn't get rid of the cloud that hung over her, at least not until lunch. *'După ploie, vine soare'* and this time it came from a completely unexpected source. Pudding was lemon tart.

The tart itself was pretty average, perhaps not even as good as that, but suddenly Maria had lemons on her mind again. The memories were sweet. Literally. Maria thought about her grandmother and all the lemon-based treats she produced – freshly squeezed lemonade, snow-white cake, and topping them all, those delicious lemon and cheese-filled pastries, Branzoaice. Maria decided she was going to do some baking on Saturday. Baking always cheered her up. The good mood engendered by her latest plan lasted the rest of the afternoon. Even the couple of hours after the children had gone home when Maria filled out assessments and generally wallowed in admin, usually the worst part of the day for her, didn't spoil it.

Back at York Way Estate, Maria discovered the lift was broken. Again. For Maria, it was no surprise. This was the third time in the last two months. There was no point making a fuss. It wouldn't change anything. She was just going to have to use the stairs to get to her flat.

As she trudged her way towards the eighth floor, Maria had plenty of time to wonder if she should look for a new flat. Perhaps she could find somewhere with a more reliable lift or, failing that, somewhere on a lower floor. But that would mean giving up the view from her bedroom window and moving away from all the local green spaces she enjoyed (weather permitting) so much. Besides, based on the stories she heard from colleagues, she might end up with a landlord a lot worse than Mr Fernandes. '*Mai bine cunoscut rău decât bine de știut,*' she thought. Although probably it wasn't appropriate to refer to Mr Fernades as a devil.

Mr Fernades was in his seventies or eighties. Like Maria, he had arrived in London with nothing to his name. Somehow, over thirty years, he had saved up enough to put down deposits on a couple of small flats. Now he relied on the income from these to supplement his pension.

Mr Fernandes had always been a good landlord. It wasn't his fault about the communal areas. That was just a part of living in an ex-council block. But if there was ever a problem in the flat, he dealt with it promptly and without cutting corners. Just as important, he hadn't raised the rent since she moved in three and a half years ago. No, better sit put. Climbing eight floors a few times a month wasn't the worst thing in the world. Besides, even if she felt exhausted by the time she arrived, looking through the window always put her back in a good mood. No, there was no way she was going to move if she didn't have to.

Maria eventually got to the eighth floor, went to her door and turning the key felt the relief of arriving home after a long day. Or at least, the relief of arriving back at the place she lived. Although she had moved to Islington five years ago, she still didn't think of London as home.

After hanging up her coat, the first thing Maria did, as she had done every day since moving into the flat, was to walk towards the window. At first, it had been the view that had drawn her in that direction. Now it was her babies. All five of them spent their entire lives in front of that south-easterly-facing window drawing in as much of the weak English sunshine as they could. The oldest had come into the world a little more than three years old, just after Maria moved into the flat. The youngest had unfolded its first leaf just a few days ago.

Each of the lemon plants (only the oldest two could really be called trees) lived in their own appropriately sized pot. In the morning, rushing to work, all Maria could do for them was to switch on a specially positioned lamp to give them a little bit of extra light while she was out. Now she would give her babies some proper attention.

For Maria, those five small living things were much more than plants. They were a central part of her identity, the focus of her life outside school, a link to her past and the important places in it. As a young girl, Maria had devoured books about lemons as avidly as she had devoured the goodies her grandmother made from them. She had learned early on that lemons were introduced to Romania, from China two thousand years ago. Discovering the exotic origin of something that was now so commonplace thrilled her. It was even more exciting to find out that for centuries, they had been synonymous with luxury and privilege, growing only in the gardens of the patrician elite. Now she had her own lemon trees growing here in her little patch of N7. It almost made her feel royal.

As Maria walked over to the window to check how her babies were doing, she couldn't help feeling a little nervous. *Was today the day?* It was the oldest of her babies that was the focus of her attention. *Was there to be a coming of age?* Peering down she could see the answer was "Da". There, fully open, was the plant's first flower. With regular watering, a bit of feeding, and plenty of light (the hardest of the three), in six months (four months if she was lucky) she would have a ripe lemon. Her very own, home-grown lemon. A lemon straight from her childhood summers. '*Răbdarea este rasplatita*'

The rest of Maria's evening was unexceptional. A TV dinner, featuring her trademark fluffy rice, another couple of hours in front of the TV and then off to bed.

Maria went to sleep content. '*Fericirea nu este ceva gata făcut. Ea vine din faptele tale,*' she thought.

Despite the English weather, despite the eight floors of stairs to be climbed and despite all the irritations of work, she had made a good day for herself. A day with lemon blossom. A happy day.

A ripe lemon next. Just another 180 days to wait. If the light was good, 60 less than that.

Superstar

The final was over. The presentation ceremony was underway. 17,000 people in the O2 Arena and millions more on TV were all watching John as he stood at the side of the court. In place of the tennis racquet that played such a central role in his life, John's hands now grasped the ATP Finals Trophy with the same firm grip. Replete with long blue ribbons hanging from its handles, the most prestigious prize in the world of indoor tennis flashed under the bright lights. Looking at the distinctive octagonal form of the elongated cup, John's thoughts took him back to his childhood.

Although it was on the other side of the globe and a lifetime ago, the country club at Runaway Bay, remained a vivid memory. It was there his tennis journey had begun. When his parents left for London, it had become both a place of work and a home for him. For a fourteen-year-old brought up in the back streets of Kingston, the club was a little piece of paradise. The immaculate lawns, the cool verandas and above all the wealth and elegance of the members in their tennis whites all spoke of a world in which perfection was possible.

Although they intersected, the members' world and John's world were very different. Any enjoyment he got from the club's facilities was entirely vicarious. His purpose in life was to ensure that the General Manager's mini-Eden remained unblemished. Every day, he diligently carried out the series of tasks assigned to him – sweeping the paths, cutting the lawns, and picking up any bits of litter that threatened the idyll. At night, he slept in a small undecorated room in the concrete outhouse that was the servants' quarters.

John had no complaints. Most of the jobs he was asked to do were tolerable and one turned out to be a pure pleasure. If you asked him, John wouldn't have been able to explain why working as a ballboy was such a joy. It wasn't something he thought about. But the time he spent on court was, without any doubt, the best thing in his life. Crouching by the side of the net, he was the most attentive spectator any player could wish to have. Half hypnotised by the rhythm of a long baseline rally, the exhilaration of an ace or the elegance of a carefully crafted drop shot, John would avidly watch every stroke of every point in every game. He noticed each shuffle of feet and every adjustment of grip. He noticed the way a wide serve opened up the court and how getting to the net enabled a player to finish a point off quickly. When John was watching tennis, time distorted. A two or three-hour match seemed to be over almost before it started.

You might have thought that fascinated as he was by tennis, John would have harboured a desire to play himself. But that thought never entered his head. Playing tennis was something members did, not something for the servants. The time he spent collecting and redistributing balls gave him a chance to peak into the members' world in the same way a passer-by might get an insight into a neighbour's life by looking through their window, but it didn't make him part of that world, and he never thought it would until that Wednesday evening.

Over the months that John had worked in the country club, he had come to have his favourite players. He marvelled at the strength of powerhouses who slammed down serves like shots from a gun and then followed up with a volley at the net and the control of players who could dominate a game with a series of carefully crafted shots whilst hardly moving from the centre of the court. But, of all the players he watched the one John idolised above all others was the owner of the club, Mr Perry. The General Manager had told John that Mr Perry had been the best player in the world when he was younger. John believed him.

Although it wasn't huge, Mr Perry's serve was the most reliable John had seen. He never gave away double faults and somehow, without using power, he managed to place his deliveries so that opponents found themselves under pressure from the start of each point. Once the ball was in play, Mr Perry, even though he was no longer a young man, would charge from side to side of the court like a golden retriever chasing after a stick. Somehow, he always managed to get to the ball. Never changing his grip, he sliced on the backhand and didn't hit big on the forehand. But then, when the opportunity came, he would pounce, running onto a ball he would swat it like a ping-pong ball, angling a volley out of the side of the court or leaping into the air to deliver an unreturnable smash.

Even if his movement was magical and some of his shots spectacular, there was something else that set Mr Perry apart from the rest of the players – his supreme confidence. Somehow, from the moment he stepped onto the court, John could sense that Mr Perry expected to win. It wasn't bluster or arrogance. It was something much stronger, calm, and deep-seated, an almost unconscious unquestioning belief in himself.

Mr Perry lived somewhere abroad and wasn't a very frequent visitor to Runaway Bay. So, John rarely got a chance to see him play. When Mr Perry was at the Club and playing tennis, John wanted, more than ever, to be on ballboy duty. Unfortunately, Wednesday was John's day off so, although John would have willingly volunteered for the duty, somebody else was ballboy that day.

John knew he was not supposed to spend time in the club grounds on his day off. Nobody wanted to see a young servant hanging around doing nothing or, worse still, doing something he shouldn't be doing. So, John was more than a little nervous when he crept into the clump of bushes by the court and lay down on his stomach. He watched the entire match without moving.

When it was over, John thought about crawling away but decided it safer to stay put until the players had disappeared into the clubhouse. That didn't happen. Instead of heading away from the bush where John was hiding, Mr Perry, still carrying his racquet, started to walk directly towards it. John thought about making a dash for it but instead remained frozen. When he was a few feet away, Mr Perry spoke. "Come out from under there."

John emerged.

Mr Perry recognised him, "It's John isn't it?" John confirmed with a nod. "What were you doing under there? Watching the match?" This time John managed a "Yes, sir." "Enjoy tennis, do you?"

John confirmed again with a more enthusiastic, "Yes, sir!" He was beginning to think he might not be in trouble.

"Well, you are right to," said Mr Perry. "It's a great sport and if you're lucky you get paid to play." After a pause, gesturing at the courts and the clubhouse, he added, "It gave me all this. Not bad for a cotton weaver's son from Stockport. Eh?" John wasn't sure he fully understood, but he nodded his head once again. Then Mr Perry asked, "Do you play?"

This time John replied with, "No, sir."

"Well, if you enjoy watching so much, you should try. Do you have a racquet?"

John gave another reply, "No, sir."

"Well, now you do," said Mr Perry, handing his racquet to John. "Take it and play. With a bit of talent and enough practise, you can achieve anything. Look at me, I wasn't the type of chap they wanted at Wimbledon, but I won it. Wouldn't look me in the eye when they gave me the club tie, wished the other chap had won but there was nothing they could do about it. I'd earned the right on the court. I was the best."

The conversation over, Mr Perry turned around and headed towards the clubhouse. As he went, he asked himself, "If they hated me winning, how would they react to a ball boy from Runaway Bay doing the same?" As he reached the veranda, Mr Perry was smiling.

John's head was in a spin. Instead of a rebuke for illicitly watching the match, he had been given a tennis racquet. John still wasn't sure he understood all of Mr Perry's comments. It didn't matter. He wasn't in trouble. More importantly, he had been given an idea. An idea that would never have come into his head of its own accord. One day he might play tennis for money, just like Mr Perry.

Of course, John knew that day wouldn't be soon. While he worked at the club, he would never go onto a court for any reason other than to crouch at the side of the net and distribute balls. He would never be a member at Runaway Bay so he would never play on their courts. But, perhaps, when it was eventually time to join his parents in London…Hadn't they said London was a town of opportunity? In the meantime, he would practise.

John fished half a dozen discarded balls from a rubbish bin and found a piece of chalk. He used it to draw a line, the height of a net on the back wall of the servants' quarters. Now he could practise. And practise he did. Every minute of John's free time was spent, racquet in hand, hitting balls against that wall.

A year later, when the call came from his parents and John left Runaway Bay for the journey to London, that same racquet was carefully packed into his suitcase.

John took a while to adjust. It wasn't just the weather and the cold. So much else was different. The grimy streets of Brixton could not contrast more with the Runaway Bay Country Club, but John felt out of place in both. London wasn't exactly welcoming. Most people ignored him. Some stared at him or made comments as we walked down the street. Once, when he sat down next to an elderly man on the bus, the man got up and moved to another seat. His parents were also nervous. Life for young people in London wasn't easy. So, they were relieved when John managed to find a job and equally pleased that John continued to spend his spare time the same way he had at Runaway Bay – hitting tennis balls against a wall.

One day, on his way home, John nodded off and missed his stop. When he pushed his sleepy eyes half-open the bus was passing the entrance to Burgess Park. There, just inside the park, John saw something that woke him up as effectively as an electric shock – tennis courts. Turning to his neighbour, John asked, "What are those courts, is there a tennis club here?"

"No," he was told, "they are public courts." The concept wasn't one that John was familiar with. Once he grasped it, John's imagination started to race once again. It was possible to play tennis without being a member of a club. No need to pay a prohibitive membership fee. An ordinary person, like him, could play tennis if they wanted. And John did want to play.

Now all John's spare time was spent on the Burgess Park courts. True, the faded lines were hard to see and the surface uneven, there was no clubhouse, not even a toilet but they were still tennis courts and John had the run of them. He could practise serves or placing the ball into a corner whenever he wanted and for as long as he wanted.

Honing his skills, John started to play matches against the other players who hung out at the courts. With his natural talent, the level of his tennis quickly improved. John started to enter competitions. At first, his success was mixed. His self-taught strokes didn't have the elegance or effectiveness of his professionally coached opponents. John didn't give up. He just worked harder. John had a good brain and an even better eye. He watched and he practised, and he learnt. It paid off. He was soon producing beautiful strokes with heavy topspin and punchy volleys. As his results improved, he entered larger and larger tournaments. Eventually, he was playing at the very top levels of the amateur game and getting results.

John started to think about the possibility of turning professional. To earn his living doing what he enjoyed most would be a blessing. But was it possible? John ran over everything in his mind. Three things concerned him the most.

At the top of the list was his height. As a child, John had been short. Now he was an adult, he was still short. That mattered when it came to serving. However high he tossed the ball and however high he leapt off the ground, five foot eight John was never going to match the power of a six foot six giant. John compensated by concentrating on placement, his sliced serves consistently landing spot on their target. That worked on the amateur circuit, and although it would be hard, John was confident he could make it work on the professional. After all, that's how Mr Perry had played.

A second issue was money. That was harder to resolve. Earning his keep from tennis had been a dream since his conversation with Mr Perry, but the adult John was realistic enough to know that life as a professional was expensive. Equipment, travel, and entry fees, it all added up. If the prize money covered it, well and good. If not, you were running a loss-making business and that's exactly what most professionals did, at least at the start of their career. They all needed some sort of financial backing. John had no rich family to support him. No sponsor to subsidise him. So, how would he live? John had a plan – he would give lessons part-time.

The sound of the MoC starting to talk brought John back to the here and now. "Presenting the trophy is our Unknown Superstar of tennis, John Bolton. Tonight, we recognise John and the forty-plus years he has devoted to tennis in his local community. His tireless efforts have resulted in the improvement of facilities using lottery and council funds. Local courts have been resurfaced and changing facilities for players have been installed. More importantly, over the years he has turned over 3,000 inner-city kids into young tennis players. In doing so, has provided them the opportunity to shine. Many have gone on to make tennis their lives, several have won sports scholarships, and others have turned professional. Please put your hands together…"

Yes, thought John as the sound of clapping filled the arena, *hearing that is good. But presenting a trophy is no substitute for winning one. Should I have turned professional?* John went back, once again, to the biggest decision in his life and the third issue which had finally settled it for him. Sometimes, he found it difficult to explain exactly what it was that made him concentrate on coaching and community work rather than a professional career. It was less tangible than the other hurdles he faced, but no less real for that. If pressed, he would have said it was simply a feeling he didn't belong on the English tennis circuit. The world of elite British tennis, with its traditions and strict etiquette, despite the geographical distance, was closer in ethos to Runaway Bay than the public courts of Lambeth and Southwark. John would have loved to be a part of the elite but, beautiful as they were, John somehow knew that the clubhouses of Surrey and Buckinghamshire would always be foreign territory. John would never be at home there. His parents weren't doctors, lawyers, or bankers, he had never been to prep school and most of all he wasn't white.

John thought of Mr Perry's comments the day he gave John his racquet. Now he had his own stories of being cold-shouldered, John understood what Mr Perry had meant. Mr Perry had fought and won, beating the system on the courts of Wimbledon. John decided to make his mark another way. He knew it was the right decision. When he was young, British tennis wasn't ready for somebody like him. Now perhaps it was. Perhaps one day soon, a young tennis player from John's part of south London would be an ATP Champion or earn his member's tie at Wimbledon and if John had played a part in making that happen, he really would have something to be proud of.

The Sommelier's Second Epiphany

It was the first week of January and the weather was typical for London at that time of year. Looking at a thermometer, your eyes would have told you the temperature was hovering just above zero. Your other senses would have told you your eyes were lying. The winds blowing in from the northeast and the drizzle-induced humidity made it feel much colder.

For the restaurant trade, the week after New Year is always dead. Those customers who can afford it are soaking up the sun on winter breaks. The heads, stomachs, and wallets of the rest of us are still recovering from the excesses of December. Nobody is inclined to go out. Better stay in and eat curled up, warm, in front of the TV. Tables in restaurants are empty.

The Neon Plum is an exception, it is always busy. Two Michelin stars and a place in the World's 50 Best do that. For the staff at *The Neon Plum*, there is never any let-up. No light evenings, no closing up early because the diners have finished and gone home. For them, every day is the same exacting struggle to achieve perfection. Every dish must be cooked and assembled with precision and consistency, every customer must be served with just the right balance of reverence and bonhomie. One misplaced word or one overcooked duck's breast could be the start of a downward spiral. A repeated mistake could destroy everything. Teams like the one at *The Neon Plum* know that only by working together, can they keep the restaurant on an upward trajectory. Every individual must play their part, every individual must push themselves to the boundaries of their potential. Every one of them must approach each evening as if it were a PB attempt in a marathon.

Siobhan was no exception. Quite the opposite. She had been under no illusion when she applied for the job at *The Neon Plum*. She knew it would be exhausting but she wanted it more than anything she ever had wanted before. She thought back to her interview. Everything she had done in the previous ten years, the stints in Dublin, Paris, and Barcelona, had just been preparation for this. It was a hard slog and there was a price. A price largely paid in time – late nights, lost weekends, curtailed holidays. None left over for hobbies, little for friends, and not much for love. Her private life was a disaster. It wasn't that she had never had relationships, it was just that she could never sustain them. But she told herself, that if her career was a success, it was worth it. If she got the job at *The Neon Plum*, she would have her reward, she would be at the pinnacle of her profession.

Siobhan understood it would be tougher than anything she had done before and it would take a greater toll on every other part of her life, but she also knew she would love it. For her, it was an uncontrollable craving. Just as a world-class athlete needs outstanding facilities and an exceptional coach, Siobhan needed *The Neon Plum* and is chef. *The Neon Plum* had a reputation. Its exacting environment and Chef's rigorous standards would push Siobhan to be the best she possibly could. That was all that mattered to her.

When Siobhan was told she had got the job, it took a while to sink in. Was she really the head sommelier at one of the best restaurants in the world? This was her opportunity; she was going to make a name for herself. She started by reviewing everything – the staff she would be working with, the stock of wines in the cellar, the wines that had sold best over the past year, even the arrangements for washing and drying the glasses. Now, five months into the job, she was still scrutinising every detail daily.

Siobhan's obsession was genetic. Her parents had inherited a pub from her grandparents. When they took over, it was just an ordinary pub in a small County Clare village. But they worked hard and soon the pub had a reputation for its food. Not much later, it was being called the best in the county. Then Siobhan's parents took the bold step of selling up to open a restaurant. Perched high on a nearby cliff, they called it *Cogar na Farraigea*.

The gamble paid off. From the beginning, they had known the views would be spectacular. More importantly, *Cogar na Farraigea* was also a culinary triumph. That success was founded on the partnership Siobhan's parents enjoyed both in the restaurant and at home. For most of the day Jack, lurked in the kitchen, frown lines puckering his forehead, as he directed operations and designed new dishes. Occasionally, he would emerge, imperious, to talk to a grateful customer. The rest of the time, front of house was Grace's domain. Grace had a knack for dealing with customers, quickly assessing the extent and tone of interaction that suited each and then using her natural charm to raise smiles. Grace's other personality, the strict disciplinarian, only showed itself when she had to discuss a misplaced fork, or heaven forbid, a drop of spilt wine, with the waiting staff.

Once a week, after six days of unrelenting concentration, Siobhan's parents had a day off. They relaxed into their home personae. Jack, happy as a child, let his *joie de vivre* run unchecked. He was the genial, bubbling centre of the family, spoiling his wife and daughters and making every Sunday feel like Christmas. Grace, for that single day, felt no imperative to control everything around her. Instead, she was content to be swept wherever her husband's whirlwind energy took them. Her only duty, cooking for the family.

They say that in family businesses, enthusiasm often dies in the third generation. In Siobhan's case, the opposite was true. How could it be any different when the most vivid memory of her childhood was the time *Cogar na Farraigea* received its first star? The entire family had celebrated for a week. In a happy childhood, Siobhan couldn't remember any other occasion that filled her with greater joy. The thought of a life that didn't revolve around a restaurant never entered her head.

As soon as she was old enough, Siobhan started to work at *Cogar na Farraigea*. Under her father's strict instruction, she cleaned vegetables and scaled fish. She had inherited his palette and quickly developed an ability to analyse which flavours and textures combined. Front of house, she learnt to lay places, polish silverware, and put customers at ease. She loved it all. She was going to help make *Cogar na Farraigea* the best restaurant in Ireland. Today, even after all those years, her ambition remained the same.

Tonight was an important step on that journey. It was the first night of *The Neon Plum*'s new menu.

Chef changed the menu four times a year, allowing him to feature the best produce of each season. With it, the wine offerings also had to change. Most importantly, the wine pairings for the tasting menu had to change.

As Siobhan knew from her careful analysis of sales, close to ninety-five percent of the customers at *The Neon Plum* took the tasting menu. This was Chef's showcase: a set seven-course meal that highlighted his creative ability and acted as a manifesto for his philosophy of cooking. *The Neon Plum* offered a wine pairing with it. Guests who took that option, and more than half did, got a different glass of wine with every course. It was part of Siobhan's job, one of the two most important parts of her job, to select those wines. It was a given that each must work with the food it was to accompany. Where Siobhan was expected to show her skill was by selecting something that would make the guests sit up and think. There were many ways of doing that. Of course, the simplest was to select a truly exceptional wine, but that didn't really require much skill or imagination. Picking an unusual or quirky wine, or making an unexpected pairing was much harder and therefore more enjoyable. At the same time, it involved more risk. But that didn't daunt Siobhan. Mastering the challenge was something Siobhan was going to have to do four times a year if she was going to excel in her profession and that was exactly what she planned to do.

This was Siobhan's second change of menu at *The Neon Plum*. The first had come soon after she started. It had been simultaneously the most stressful and most exciting moment of Siobhan's career to date. She felt like an athlete who had made it to an Olympic final – hard work had got her that far, now she faced the ultimate test. Of course, Siobhan had been through menu changes before, but this was different. Now she was responsible. She needed to prove herself. She had to ensure that each of the seven pairings was perfect.

Siobhan knew it would take time, but she was ready to put the hours in. And she did. For a month, Siobhan lived at *The Neon Plum*. Course by course, Siobhan worked her way through the menu. First, she ate Chef's creations with no accompaniment, savouring the flavours, textures, and look of the dish. After that, she spoke to Chef asking him about the dish; the ingredients, his inspiration and, most importantly, what he wanted to achieve. Only then did she start to think about which wines to select. For each course, she considered every potential wine in the restaurant's cellar and a fair few that were not. For each course, she made three selections, her preferred choice, and two alternatives that she liked less but thought could also work – twenty-one wines in total.

The reckoning was next. Every member of staff was to have the chance to try each dish with each of the three pairings she had made. Without knowing her preferences, they would provide feedback during an open discussion. Siobhan was more nervous than Judas at the Last Supper. She was being judged. Although the comments her colleagues made were reasoned and constructive and nothing was said in malice, the experience was still bitter-sweet.

Siobhan loved few things more than discussing wines. At the same time, she felt vulnerable. She had opened herself up, her professionalism, that central part of her being was open to criticism. She knew the words she was hearing could easily wound her. At the end of the session, Chef sat down with

Siobhan to make the final choices. Five of Siobhan's preferences received unanimous approval and went onto the menu. Chef replaced two with second-choice alternatives.

Siobhan wasn't sure how to take the outcome. Overall, Chef seemed pleased. At the same time, even after all the hours she had put in, Siobhan felt she had failed on two out of the seven. She had made the wrong selections, if she had selected correctly, they would have been universally approved. That also meant that the choices that had been approved might just be the best of a bad trio.

Of course, it was the guests' opinion and not that of her colleagues that really counted. So, opening night for the new menu was a second trial for Siobhan. The final verdict on her selections would come with the guests' feedback.

Getting that feedback required effort on Siobhan's part. Most guests said nothing about the wines unless prompted. When she did, the responses were, in most cases, nothing more than a blandly positive "nice" "lovely" or "very nice." On the rare occasion, a guest expressed an opinion that said something about the wine or pairing, Siobhan listened intently. In general, Siobhan was content with what she heard. She wanted to please the guests and a guest who discovered something new, who was surprised that an unexpected combination worked or who simply delighted in something that brought back memories, was a happy customer. On the rare occasion that a guest criticised something, Siobhan took it to heart. Particularly, when she recognised some truth in the comment.

The guest who thought the selection for the second fish course was an excellent wine but overpowered the food, the diner who thought the sugar levels in the Spätlese weren't high enough to match Chef's desert, and the one who simply thought the Barbaresco was over-oaked all confirmed what Siobhan already knew. She had not achieved perfection with her choice of pairings for the first change of menu.

Sitting in the staff room at the end of an evening after one of the guests had made a particularly cutting remark, Siobhan thought back to a conversation with her father ten years earlier. She had just finished her course at a catering college in Galway and was back home waiting to graduate. She expected and would have been perfectly content, to continue her life as it had been before she left for college. So, it was a shock for Siobhan when her parents refused to let her into the restaurant. Explaining the decision, Jack said, "You are not ready yet. You know nothing that will take *Cogar na Farraigea* to the next level. If you want a job here, go away, work in the best restaurants in Europe, learn everything you can and only come back when you can help us get our second star!" Sensing her parent's ambition for her and faced with an unyielding refusal to employ her, Siobhan left.

I'm still not ready, thought Siobhan, *I've still got so much to learn, I'm still making mistakes.* It was then that she noticed Chef coming towards her. In Chef's presence, Siobhan usually pulled on the bright and cheerful service persona she had learned from her mother. That evening, perhaps because she was tired, perhaps because she was still thinking about the guest's comments, Siobhan couldn't do it. Chef noticed the difference instantly and Siobhan had no option but to tell him what had upset her.

After hearing her out, Chef responded by telling her a story. "As you know," he began, "near the beginning of my career, I worked in Tokyo. When I was there, I heard about what everybody in Tokyo said was the best Sushi restaurant in the world. I had to visit it. It took me six months to get a seat but, eventually, I did."

"The restaurant was tiny, more a bar than a restaurant, and the décor far from special. But the sushi was spectacular. I watched as each piece was prepared in front of me. They were simple, delicately flavoured, and brilliantly crafted. I will never forget that meal. It has shaped everything I have done since. But what really made that visit the most important experience of my career was my conversation with the owner of the bar."

"He was a sixth-generation Sushi Chef, already in his eighties. Of course, I had read everything I could about him before I visited. So, I knew that he supervised every detail from the buying of fish at the market to the cooking of the rice and the construction of each piece presented in his restaurant. When I had the chance, I asked him how he achieved such perfection. Do you want to know what his response was? He said he hadn't achieved perfection, that he would never achieve perfection but that he would always keep on trying. I must have looked puzzled because he went on to say that, five years earlier, he had realised that everything he had done before was worthless precisely because he had expected to eventually achieve perfection. When he had realised perfection was not possible, not in life, not in art, and not in cooking, his work had improved. Now it was better than it had been five years ago and in another five years, it would be even better, but it would never be perfect. Seeking perfection without expecting to achieve it was the only way to improve."

"And you know what, he's right."

"If you expect to achieve perfection, you have chosen the wrong profession. You should have been a mathematician. In a restaurant, perfection is impossible. Yes, there are rules and if you follow them, you can create great things. If you know the rules and how to break them, you may achieve the exceptional. But although you must aspire to perfection, you must also know you will never achieve it. For one thing, you are dealing with people and no two people want the same things. Nothing you do will please them all."

Chef's story was a moment of enlightenment for Siobhan. Accepting that she could never achieve perfection was liberating. It allowed her to look at her work in another way. Now, the comments of the double jury of peers and customers were not something to dread, they were not a sign of failure, now each one of them was just something that could help her to improve.

Siobhan worked even harder on her second menu change than she had on the first. She spent more time at the restaurant, researched a wider range of pairings, and agonised even more than the first time about her choices. Eventually, she made her selection. Twenty wines, and in a nod to Chef's story, an aged honjozo sake to go with Chef's favourite dish on the menu, the scallops. The choice was characteristically bold, but it wasn't made for show. Siobhan knew that nothing else would enhance the caramelised sweetness and accentuate the velvety umami flavour of the scallops better than this sake. It was a bonus that its nuttiness added further character to the match and brought out the flavours in the hazelnut butter.

This time, Siobhan's work received almost unreserved approval from her colleagues. Six of her seven top picks, including the sake, which Chef loved with the scallops, made it onto the menu. But now the real test was imminent. She was going to find out if she had really managed to get any closer to perfection. The first guests were arriving.

As the maître d'or led the party through the restaurant, Siobhan took the opportunity to study them. It always helped to have an idea of who she would be talking to before she arrived at their table. For Siobhan, the most important part of her job, after the initial selection of wines, was the presentation of those wines to the guests. Dining at a restaurant like *The Neon Plum* was about more than the food, it should be an experience. How the food and drink were presented could make the difference for a guest between a good evening and an exceptional one. Siobhan would never forget the theatrical quality of her first and only visit to Heston Blumenthal's *Fat Duck* – the visual trickery of the orange and beetroot jellies and clouds of smoke coming from the liquid nitrogen the serving staff used to create bacon and egg ice cream in front of her, encapsulated it all. Every guest at *The Neon Plum* was expected to have an equally exceptional evening.

So it was good there was something of the show woman in Siobhan. Back at *Cogar na Farraigea*, when she was old enough, Siobhan had enjoyed serving the wine more than anything else. There was something almost sacred in the ceremony of telling the guest about each bottle, its origin, the grapes that had gone into it, and the heritage of the vinery that had produced it. Then pausing to let them taste it before finally pouring out the full glasses. It reminded Siobhan of mass in St Mary's only not as solemn and with an audience full of genuine anticipation. Every time she conducted the ceremony, she felt herself a pagan priestess, powerful and all-knowing as she cared for those she served.

Siobhan had been working hard on the presentation patter for the pairing menu. Both she and her assistant had practised it extensively. Tonight, they were going to put it into practice for the first time.

Her experience, training, and research meant Siobhan could have talked for hours about any of the wines on the menu. She knew the characteristics of each grape and each region. She knew which regions had produced good wines in which years and how long to wait before drinking them. More than that, she knew everything there was to know about each individual vineyard and vintner – which way the vineyards faced, the soil they stood on, what they were producing, why they were producing it, and what they wanted to achieve in the future. She had visited almost all of them and had long conversations with the owners on exactly these topics. But Siobhan knew that even die-hard wine buffs had a limit to how much talk they could stand. She wanted to avoid the encyclopaedic monologues of the head sommelier she had worked for in Dublin. They inevitably ended with the guests' eyes glazing over before they took their first sip of wine.

Siobhan had made it clear at her interview that her mission at *The Neon Plum* would be to entertain. She wanted the guests to be intrigued by the wines they were drinking, to think about why they worked (or didn't work) with the food, and to ask questions. Her strategy was to keep the facts in the initial patter to a bare minimum and to roll out additional information about the wine only if the guests asked. Instead, Siobhan trained herself and her assistant to talk about the pairings. Sometimes, she let the guests know the reason she had chosen a wine when she presented it, explaining its qualities and why she thought it worked with a particular dish. For other pairings, especially some of the bolder ones, Siobhan wanted to surprise the guests and only explain the reasons for her choice after she had been able to ask their thoughts. Siobhan's approach created more interaction with the guests and, that for her was good. She had always thought that getting a conversation going with the guests who wanted it was one of the most important parts of the job. The policy was certainly a step up from the Dublin approach. But even so, Siobhan was not completely satisfied. She wasn't getting through to all the guests. She needed something more.

The first group were almost at their table, Table 2. Judging by the way they were dressed, they had come straight from work. If she had to put money on it, Siobhan would have guessed that the man confidently striding in front was the boss and the others tagging behind his subordinates. *Perhaps,* Siobhan thought, *a team celebrating a big achievement.*

Other guests were arriving. Table 15 was two women. A mother and daughter thought Siobhan and by the way, they were talking, they hadn't seen each other for a while. Table 20, two businessmen discussing a deal. Tables 4 and 8 were both middle-aged married couples. Table 7, parents with a teenage daughter. Table 1, an older gentleman with a younger woman, clearly not his daughter.

Siobhan brought the wine menu to Table 2 and asked if they wanted any drinks while they were waiting. The man she had identified as the boss spoke for the table. Champagne all round to start, the wine pairing to go with the meal and a couple of bottles of fizzy water. *Yes,* thought Siobhan, *a work celebration and it is clear who is enjoying it most of all!*

Tables 15 and 20 ordered wines by the bottle while Table 7 declined alcohol altogether. *Less work on those three tables*, thought Siobhan. Table 1 was another champagne and wine pairing, while Table 4 went for vodka-martinis and the pairing. Table 8 chose the pairing but no aperitif. "The pairing itself would be plenty," said the wife.

Siobhan helped the tables ordering wine to select something that matched their food choices. Table 20 had ordered a la carte. That made it a pretty routine task and one Siobhan had been through countless times in her career. Table 15 had decided to go for the tasting menu without the pairing. That was a challenge. How could one wine truly match all seven of Chef's creations? Even though Siobhan had some ready-prepared suggestions, and the two women she was helping were happy to be guided by her, the final choice was inevitably going to be a bit of a compromise. Siobhan reckoned that wines for this universal role should display bright fruit flavours, good acidity, and low tannin. Siobhan's approach, to spice things up a bit, had been to look for fresher versions of wines that were traditionally big and bold. The final choice came down to a New Zealand Pinot Noir and an Argentinian Malbec. The women went with the Pinot Noir.

As the tables taking the pairing option started to receive their first courses, Siobhan and her assistant swung into action with the carefully rehearsed patter she had prepared. This was the first opportunity for Siobhan to get any indication of how interested each table was going to be in what she had to say.

It was obvious that the couple at Table 1 were more interested in each other than anything Siobhan had to say. She would keep her comments to a minimum. The dynamic on Table 2 was more complex. The boss clearly enjoyed having

Siobhan stand in front of him and do her piece for him. He carefully interjected with a few comments to display his knowledge. But when she had finished her set piece and was ready for questions, all he wanted to hear was more of his own voice. The rest of the table was harder to judge. Siobhan thought she saw a spark or two of interest in some of their eyes, but they remained silent throughout and only became animated again when their boss started to talk.

Table 4 listened politely to what she had to say, but she sensed no real enthusiasm. Table 8 was different. Siobhan could see from the way they lent slightly towards her that they were listening to every word she uttered and the questions they asked showed they were interested in everything she was imparting. Siobhan instantly knew Table 8 was going to be her favourite that evening.

Taking away the glasses after the first course, Siobhan asked the couple what they thought of the wine, an Eva Fricke creation that was her favourite Riesling Trocken. "I'm a sucker for a good Riesling," said the husband, "and I thought that was a good one."

"And the pairing?" asked Siobhan.

"Great together," said the wife, "fresh and bright like a newly married couple." Siobhan left with a quiet smile on her face.

The scallop and sake combination that followed was another success. Just as Siobhan had expected. This time the guests compared the pairing to a film romance. An unexpected love affair that after a few twists turns out to be perfect and is immortalised forever. This time as Siobhan took away the glasses, she had an even bigger smile on her face.

The next course was one of Chef's more exuberant offerings. Monkfish presented with a medley of flavours and textures including truffle oil, fruit, and nuts. When Siobhan poured the wine, she gave the guests her full spiel explaining it was an amber wine from Georgia, mentioning the vintner, saying a bit about the unusual production process, and outlining some of the wine's main characteristics. She said nothing about the pairing. It was another of her surprise combinations.

When the couple finished the course, Siobhan asked, "Did you enjoy the wine?"

"To be honest," said the wife, "when I first tried it, I was disappointed. I didn't think it was anything special, a bit bland. But when I had it with the food, I liked it. I'm not sure I understand what your chef was aiming for with the dish, but it's complex. There can't be many wines that would cope with all the different flavours! I would say the wine was like a clever woman who has the patience and understanding to support an eccentric genius and help him to shine." Siobhan chuckled out loud, the comment was spot on. She had struggled more than usual to find a wine to match this creation of Chef's wild imagination, and in the end, she had settled for something that wasn't going to be a star itself but would support the dish. This Georgian Amber coped with the array of flavours, more than that, it brought them to the front, especially the earthiness of the truffles.

Thinking of clever men brought Javier to mind. Of all Siobhan's romantic relationships, the longest lasting was with Javier. It had started when she was working in Barcelona. They had met at a wine festival and then at a series of tastings over the next few months. During those meetings, Siobhan discovered that, just as she was a third-generation restaurateur, he was a third-generation vintner. That wasn't all they had in common. Both were passionate about their work, appreciating tradition but focused on innovation and pushing out boundaries. Siobhan was in the middle of a campaign to introduce new wines at the restaurant where she worked, her first job as a head sommelier. Javier, who had a winery in Galicia, was experimenting with Mencia to produce light, perfumed reds. Siobhan adored the results and had fallen in love with Javier's wines long before she met him. So, it was no surprise she was happy to spend hours listening to his monologues about grapes and wine-making techniques. For his part, Javier was always happy to have an audience. He was knowledgeable, had such clear ideas on what the industry needed, and spoke with such authority that Siobhan felt she was learning something every minute she was with him.

Her appetite whetted, Siobhan was looking forward to hearing what the couple had to say on the pairing for the next course. The comments were not what she had hoped for, "It didn't quite work for me. I couldn't help thinking of a couple who have been together for a while and are about to break up." In line with her new philosophy, Siobhan took the criticism well. Was there some truth in what the guests were saying? Thinking about it, she had to admit there was something in the pairing that reminded her of her last few months with Javier. One evening, listening to Javier declaiming about his mission to change the image of Spanish wines, Siobhan realised she was bored. She had heard it all before. When Javier talked, he was still as enthusiastic and earnest as he had always been. But she had grown. Now, for her, there was nothing fresh about anything he said and, after twelve months of seeing him, Siobhan knew Javier had no other topics of conversation. This pairing had been equally boring.

In contrast, the crispy pork and champagne combination was "a masterstroke, like a wild love affair". Siobhan, who, by now, was thinking about her own relationships as much as the wine and food, remembered Paris and Pierre. Siobhan had had her doubts about that one from the start. She had come to expect a certain kind of customer to flirt with her and had developed a slick technique for brushing them off firmly but without offence. With Pierre, it didn't work. He was different. He didn't give up and, when Siobhan was honest with herself, she admitted she didn't really want him to. Even though he must have been twenty years older than her, he was still handsome, soaked in charm, and had dark intense eyes that undermined her resolve. Eventually, she gave way and scribbled down her number on a scrap of paper.

For the next three weeks, her love life was as intense as her work life. Time distorted. Living in their warped reality Siobhan and Pierre managed to visit clubs, theatres and, of course, restaurants all over Paris as well as spending a lot of time in bed. But, even before the night, she saw him on the Metro with a woman who was clearly his wife, Siobhan knew that Pierre, sparkling and exciting as he was, would only be a brief episode in her life. The guests never knew those wonderful times with Pierre were the reason for the happy look in Siobhan's eyes.

The pairing for the final savoury course, the Hardwick Lamb was, according to Table 8, "a couple who have been together for thirty years". "And that's a bad thing?" asked Siobhan.

"No," came the answer, "they know each other perfectly, thirty years together may not be exciting, but it's stood the test of time and that makes it a classic." *This one's my parents*, thought Siobhan.

When Siobhan came to collect the glasses after the couple's final course she was at once anxious to hear what they had to say and a little sad that she would be listening to the last metaphor of the evening. "Well?" she asked.

"First love," came the response. "Both equally matched in sweetness and passion, as close as you can come to perfection, but how long will it last?"

Dan, thought Siobhan. Blonde-haired and always smiling, Dan had been a classmate at catering college. He was the kindest boy she ever met. More than that, there was something about Dan that reminded Siobhan of her father on his days off. He babbled nonsense to her, gave her flowers and brought her breakfast in bed. It had all worked so well when they were in Galway. But with her in Dublin and him in Cork (he had found a trainee chef position there), things were harder. At first, there had been intense telephone conversations in the early hours of the morning and surprise visits when he arrived unannounced on his day off. But, with time, things went the way of so many long-distance relationships. Siobhan immersed in her work, had less and less spare time. The calls got shorter and the visits fewer until, eventually, amongst many tears, Siobhan had called the whole thing off.

Slipping back to the present, something clicked in Siobhan's mind. She suddenly felt an overwhelming desire to hug the guests in front of her. She had it. This was what she was looking for. People understand people better than they understand flavours. Even she, with all her professional knowledge was now thinking about wine pairings the way the couple were. *If part of my patter is talking about pairings, the way they do, I will be able to communicate with anybody about food and wine. A year more here honing my skills and I will have something unique to offer Cogar na Farraigea. I've got my visa back to Ireland and when I get there, I'll be calling Dan!*